5/19/01

Dear Suzi,

Happy Birthday to a special friend. I have so many wonderful memories of our high school years together. Seems like yesterday that we were eating pizza for the "first time."

I'll always remember & appreciate your mom's great cooking. Her cherry pie was the greatest.

Happy Birthday, Suzi —

Love,
Diane

The Touch
of the
Master's Hand

Also by Larry Barkdull

The Mourning Dove

The Touch
of the
Master's Hand

Larry Barkdull

Golden Books

NEW YORK

Golden Books®
888 Seventh Avenue
New York, NY 10106

Copyright © 1998 by Barkdull Publishing, LLC
Golden Books® and colophon
are trademarks of Golden Books Publishing Co., Inc.

Designed by Gwen Petruska Gürkan
Illustrations by Yan Nascimbene

Typography: Title in Wade Sans Light, Text in Weiss

Manufactured in the United States of America

10   9   8   7   6   5   4   3   2   1

Library of Congress Cataloging-in-Publication Data
Barkdull, Larry.
        The touch of the master's hand / Larry Barkdull.
               p.   cm.
        ISBN 0-307-44010-9 (hc: alk. paper)
        I. Title.
        PS3552.A6166T68   1998
        813'.54—dc 21   98-7151
                                                CIP

To
Andria Cranney
and
Phebe Kay Hawkes

ACKNOWLEDGMENTS

Grateful thanks to Ted Gibbons for allowing adaptation of his story "Legacy"; to Dr. Robert Manookin for his insights into the music; to Brian and Cheryl Crouch for help in southeastern Idaho; to my cousin Michael Olsen for living parts of this story with me; to my aunt Eddie for the character Edna Wane Widener; to the memory of Heber J. Grant, from whose youth is adapted an account in the chapter "A Test of Integrity"; to Myra Brooks Welch (1877–1959), who wrote the beautiful poem in 1921; to the Church of the Brethren for providing the original text; and to Ann Park for sharing the story of her father's sacrifice, which was the inspiration for this book.

To the little mentally handicapped girl in Mrs. Wray's 1961 fifth-grade class: please forgive childhood's thoughtlessness.

The Touch of the Master's Hand

by Myra Brooks Welch

'Twas battered and scarred, and the auctioneer
Thought it scarcely worth his while
To waste much time on the old violin,
But held it up with a smile:

"What am I bidden, good folks," he cried,
"Who'll start the bidding for me?"
"A dollar, a dollar"; then, "Two! Only two?
Two dollars, and who'll make it three?

"Three dollars, once; three dollars, twice;
Going for three—"But no,
From the room, far back, a gray-haired man
Came forward and picked up the bow;

Then, wiping the dust from the old violin,
And tightening the loose strings,
He played a melody pure and sweet
As a caroling angel sings.

The music ceased, and the auctioneer,
With a voice that was quiet and low,

Said: "What am I bid for the old violin?"
And he held it up with the bow.

"A thousand dollars, and who'll make it two?
Two thousand! And who'll make it three?
Three thousand, once, three thousand, twice,
And going, and gone," said he.

The people cheered, but some of them cried,
"We don't quite understand
What changed its worth." Swift came the reply:
"The touch of a master's hand."

And many a man with life out of tune,
And battered and scarred from sin,
Is auctioned cheap to the thoughtless crowd,
Much like the old violin.

A "mess of pottage," a glass of wine;
A game—and he travels on.
He's "going" once, and "going" twice,
He's "going" and almost "gone."

But the Master comes, and the foolish crowd
Never can quite understand
The worth of a soul and the change that's wrought
By the touch of the Master's hand.

CONTENTS

The Touch
of the
Master's Hand

The Nightingale

IT WASN'T AS IF I HAD never attended a concert. But this one was exceptional and I was nervous. I sat with my wife, Rebecca—Rebe, with two hard *e*'s—fidgeting like a boy on his first date.

"Shadrach Widener, stop tugging at your collar," Rebe said, poking me in the ribs and calling me by my full name. The "Shadrach" part had belonged to Grandma Widener's great-grandfather.

"Shad, did you hear me?" Rebe elbowed me again. "Leave your collar alone. I just starched it!"

Rebe is a peach. I loved her from the moment I set eyes on her. She, like I, was a soon-to-be sixth-grader at Iona Elementary. Her dimpled smile and strawberry-blond hair made young locals hope for her affection. I was one. But in those days I loved her from afar. Dad used to remind me about patience being a virtue. He was right because

Rebe is mine now—the dimples, the strawberry-blond hair, the sharp elbows, everything.

"I'm so excited to be here!" she gushed. Rebe is the music enthusiast in our family. She has other talents. She's on time, for example. A clock inside her warns of impending tardiness. She also knows how everything should be done. I learned early on that if I do things Rebe's way, that's the right way. And that's a comfort for any husband.

All told, Rebe is a woman I would not, could not, live without. Mom and Dad loved her like a daughter. When Dad died last year it was Rebe who had insisted on caring for him. She did the same for Mom, who had died ten years earlier. Dad's pension benefits from his thirty years at Zeb's Truss Joist included generous medical benefits, but Rebe wouldn't hear of a care center. She bathed him, changed him, and administered his medications to the end.

After the orchestra had tuned and quieted and the last of the audience had settled, we waited for the conductor. I thumbed through the program. "Violin Concerto in E Minor by Felix Mendelssohn." Mom would have loved this, I thought. Mendelssohn was her favorite composer. She introduced me to him in 1961 by way of a portable record player on the kitchen table.

I read on: "Jean Van Olpin—violin soloist." The program listed her accomplishments. She was called "The Nightingale" for the lyrical quality of her performance. My mother would have agreed with the superlative descriptions. Jean Van Olpin was her favorite performer. Dad's, too. Together, they followed her every performance, collected every newspaper clipping, owned every album. It was her music that had roused them each morning the way the aroma of just-baked bread can coax one from an easy chair. Both Mom and Dad requested that her music be played at their funerals. So I knew when Zeb's Truss Joist established a music endowment in my father's name, nothing would have pleased him more than to be honored with Jean Van Olpin's music. I never doubted she would come.

The house darkened. A spotlight silhouetted a solitary man who stepped onto center stage. The audience welcomed him and he bowed. Extending his hand, he motioned to stage left. The spot moved and the elegant figure of a woman emerged carrying a violin and bow.

In one motion, the audience arose and applauded. The houselights went bright then, and the conductor and orchestra joined in the ovation. Jean Van Olpin acknowledged her peers and admirers. A gesture of her hand quieted us and we returned to our seats.

I looked at Rebe and squeezed her hand.

"Are you all right?" she asked.

"Yes." But I could feel emotions well inside me. I felt unable to toughen against the flood of feelings that had wakened within me.

The houselights dimmed and the conductor raised his baton. A single light shone on Jean Van Olpin. From the first notes she drew from her instrument, I felt an electricity. Some people sat forward. She attacked each note with confidence, executing the most difficult passages with precision. But I heard past the mechanics, the style, the articulation. I closed my eyes. The music became an entity, a living, breathing soul, knocking on my senses like an old friend visiting. She and Mendelssohn had become one.

She let her bow fly over the expanse of the fingerboard then return to the theme, shifting between melody and accompaniment. Transitioning from bold, she launched soft sounds that floated overhead and wafted back to earth like a glider touching down.

I sat in a muse, transported. The music carried me to 1961. That was the year the miracles happened. I doubted Jean Van Olpin would have disagreed. She is, after all, my sister.

Throwing Rocks at Bats

JEANNIE TURNED NINE the summer after our family moved to Iona, Idaho. She didn't know about the bats. Neither did I. I was two years her senior and had just completed the fifth grade. Bats were one of the discoveries we had to make that summer to call Iona home.

Jeannie and I didn't sleep indoors during the summer of 1961. Iona's children didn't consider bunking indoors. Maybe sleeping arrangements were different in Idaho Falls, the big city five miles away. In Iona, we rotated camping in friends' backyards, but seldom slumbered. We used Dad's sleeping bags from his World War II days.

Jeannie followed me about and was accepted as one of the guys. She wasn't a *girl* then. Clad in patched denims, with short, uncombed hair, she looked more a tow-headed boy. That she could spit and fight maintained the image.

Our new friend Billy Bob, whose real name was William Robert, taught us chess that summer. We played it into the night by flashlight. Billy lived in one of Iona's basement houses—a foundation with a roof. We pretended it was a cave. An abandoned caboose parked in the side yard gave us a spot to plan adventures. Billy knew which irrigation ditches to swim on hot summer afternoons. The surrounding foothills had snakes and lizards to catch. Billy and I ferreted out the critters by making Jeannie crawl like Rin Tin Tin, the television dog. We taught her to point with her front leg curled, just like "Rinny." But she didn't do the part well and the reptiles seemed unimpressed. Cowboys and Indians was a fun game. Jeannie hated being the squaw. We didn't know any Indian war chants. Jeannie suggested "The Chipmunks Song." Oddly, we found a way to make it work.

In 1961 Iona was unaware that in three years it would be invaded by the Beatles. Our parents weren't prepared. My mother was disgusted and said Mendelssohn would be, too. We children were cautiously thrilled. Until they came, when we wanted to be daring, we basked in Elvis. Idaho's adults were pretty sure the new music was a Communist plot, and some acted out their fears by building bomb shelters. Perhaps they had reason for concern. Our community was often blasted by air raid sirens originating in Idaho Falls; our television was interrupted by the Emergency Broadcasting System; and Iona Elementary taught us to hide under our desks when the bombs fell.

In the late spring of 1961, my father, Sam Widener, had moved our family to Iona. He'd lost his business in Ucon. A white house on Main Street became our new home. It was a rental. My mother, Edna Wane Widener—Eddie to friends—loved the "White House." A childhood bout with polio had left her with a painful limp. The white house had few stairs and Mom could navigate it with relative ease. Dad hoped to buy it for her when finances improved.

Our move was tempered by Dad's bringing our tire swing from Ucon. He hung it on a limb of a large cottonwood in our front yard. That familiarity returned the sense of calm the move had taken away. And we had our parents. The world might be reeling, and houses and money might fail, but Jeannie and I could glide in the safe circle of our tire swing, secure in the knowledge that our father loved our mother and that she loved him back.

Dad was never completely without work. Being an electrician and carpenter, he found jobs to keep food on the table. As a boy I watched him, fascinated by his skill. He had learned the virtue of hard work from his father, who was the last of my grandparents to die.

When we moved to Iona, Dad gave us a quick tour. Kitty-corner from our house was the Iona Mercantile—the Merc. We stood on its steps and Dad directed our eyes across Main Street to the Stanger Memorial Building, originally a house of worship—a tabernacle. Pioneers had settled the area in 1883 and ten years later, at the site of their first camp, built the tabernacle. The countryside was bleak and treeless then, but the settlers named it Iona—Hebrew for "beautiful"—after the village in ancient Palestine.

They went right to work clearing the land and planting cottonwood trees. By 1961 Iona had lived up to its name.

Billy knew where the bats would be. He told us one dark June night.

At the end of Main stood an empty, rickety house. Its weather-worn boards, broken shutters, and weed-infested yard spoke of a Halloween scene. The yard harbored Iona's one streetlight. We approached and noticed five boys throwing rocks at the light. Their aim was terrible, I thought. None of them could hit the bulb. When I managed a better look, I realized that the light wasn't their target. With each pitch, shadowy figures darted from the dark, chased the rocks to the ground, then flew away.

Bats!

They were throwing rocks at bats!

"Watch this!" Billy hollered as he chucked a rock into the light's glow. When it peaked and turned earthward, a black bat dove at it.

"Why do they do that?" asked Jeannie.

"Bats can't see. They use radar," replied Billy like an expert. "To a bat, a rock seems like a big bug." He handed Jeannie and me some stones and said, "You try."

I threw first. I heaved a rock high into the light, but it dipped and fell with a thud.

"Hey, Brainless!" a voice called out from the dark. "You throw like a *girl*." The voice belonged to Delbert Mundy, but everyone called him "Debby." His was a name that didn't fit. I knew him. He and his father brought Dad jobs from time to time. I knew Debby was one person in Iona I should avoid.

When Debby stepped to where I could see him, close enough for me to tell he hadn't brushed his teeth in a long while, he stood six inches taller than I and had biceps. He wore his shirtsleeves rolled to his shoulders so that the muscles were visible in all their naked horror. Debby was a year older than I and cussed and smoked like my parents had warned that some junior high kids do.

I had no comeback to his evaluation of my throw. I had never joined a baseball team. I didn't own a baseball glove. Maybe he was right.

Suddenly I heard Jeannie yell, "Oh, yeah?"

It was received badly. I hadn't time to hush her before Debby walked over to me, turned to Billy and said, "Who's the jerk?" Debby didn't wait for the answer. He gave me a shove and I fell backwards over one of his cronies who had squatted behind my knees on all fours. There followed a shriek of laughter from the gang. Debby hovered over me a moment, pulled a wad of chewing gum from behind his ear, plopped it in his mouth, and said, "Bring *her* back when *she's* grown."

I felt small.

Jeannie lunged at Debby like a Doberman, but Billy held her back.

Debby laughed and spit in the street. "Some tough bodyguard!" Then he and his company crossed Main into the shadows of cottonwoods to cuss and smoke. Billy dragged Jeannie and they sat down beside me.

"You wanna go?" he asked.

"No. Maybe they'll leave in a minute." We hid behind a bush to watch.

I had seen smoking before, but not in my home, and not by someone my own age. I wondered if smoking was how Debby had grown so strong. I considered his use of profanities and wondered if I would be feared and followed if I used them.

Soon the gang found a new game. Debby had brought some frozen peas and was sticking them up his nose. As he pulled one out, he called it a green booger and chased the boys, threatening to hang it on them. We thought the game was disgusting but we watched anyway.

Suddenly, Debby began to howl. "Help me! I can't get it out!"A pea had lodged high in his nostril where his thick fingers couldn't reach. Worse, the pea had melted into mush.

"Push it down from above!" yelled one boy.

"It's too high up!" screamed Debby.

"Get a hose!" another suggested.

"He'll drown!" piped a wise one.

Then someone volunteered Jerry Craddock, the smallest boy, whose nickname sounded like someone's from the '40s. "Jeepers, you've got the littlest fingers. Dig it out!"

"Not me!" bellowed Jeepers, and tried to bolt.

"Grab him!"

Debby hacked and blew.

The older boys held Jeepers, one clutching his flailing legs, another wrestling his arm behind his back, a third guiding his pinky to Debby's nostril.

"Get him away from me!" screamed Debby.

The relieved Jeepers and his clean finger were dropped to the ground.

It had become apparent that Debby's disciples didn't know what to do. Jeannie did. She held her sides and whooped it up. The gang took notice.

"Shut up, you dork! He can't breathe," barked Jeepers.

Debby was running around trying to clear his nose like a farmer. I stood up and yelled, "Serves you right!"

It was a mistake.

Debby shook his fist and swore an oath he would get even. Then he cried, "Get me to a doctor!" And his band rushed him away.

Two things became certain that night: One, Debby would get even; and two, I *did* throw like a girl. The first was inevitable. We decided to work on the second. So every day for a week, Billy coached me in the art of throwing. To my chagrin, Jeannie picked it up instantly.

"Take a step forward with your left foot and throw past your ear! Don't push it. Throw it past your ear!" I found myself struggling with every instruction. As if attending a cocoon, Billy and Jeannie waited for a throwing technique to emerge. Finally, what was mechanical became natural. To celebrate, we decided to return to the bats.

Billy was the first to hurl a rock into the glow.

Nothing.

"You try," he urged me. I chose a rock that I supposed would resemble a delicious moth to a bat. I launched it into the light. Immediately a winged mouselike figure darted and crashed into it. The dark body fell to the ground in a heap. We admired it, then the bat recovered and flapped away. That encouraged us to try again.

Then, from inside the house where the streetlight stood, the figure of a young girl appeared in the window outlined by a dim light.

"Who's that?" whispered Jeannie.

"Oh, no! They're back!" groaned Billy.

"Who?"

"The Shimmels—Sheila Shimmel and her grandpa!"

"What's that mean?"

"No more throwing rocks at bats!"

Savvy locals knew all about the Shimmels. Billy filled us in as we walked home. Sheila's mother had died delivering her, and the midwife had dropped Sheila on her head. That's why she was crazy. Sheila's grandpa tried to cure her mind with witchcraft and chants, but nothing worked. He even smeared her face with toad guts, but it made her break out in warts the size of quarters. "When Sheila's father took one look at her," Billy continued, "he said he wouldn't be father to something that dumb and ugly." Billy said Sheila's grandpa used a knotty cane to beat her and other children he caught. Worst of all, Sheila had fleas. Jeannie and I were informed that anyone coming in contact with her would get infected. Once in Ririe she had rubbed up against someone who had to be quarantined for a month. The Shimmels came and went, but now they were back to haunt Iona.

Jeannie gazed back at the window as we walked home. "She looked lonesome."

"Lonesome like a rattlesnake!" Billy countered. "She's crazy, I tell you."

For a few days we fussed about losing the streetlight, but the infusion of insanity into our neighborhood more than replaced it. I could not have known then that Sheila's path and mine would soon converge.

Smokin' and Cussin'

WHEN BILLY AND I DECIDED TO take up smoking, each of us spit in our hands and shook on it. We reckoned that Jeannie would tell if we included her, so we kept quiet. The sign in the Merc said no cigarettes to minors. I once had heard that corn silk could be smoked instead of tobacco. We decided to stuff it in straws and that would have to do.

The Merc was the only store in town. It was an old stone building and carried food staples and some luxuries. J. D. and Elva Perkins owned the Merc. They knew my parents; they knew they didn't smoke.

When Billy and I entered the Merc, Elva greeted us and asked how were my folks, and had my mother finished sewing Jeannie's dress with the fabric Elva helped pick out?

"Just fine, Mrs. Perkins. Not yet, Mrs. Perkins," I answered.

"What'll it be today?" a voice boomed. In addition to owning the Merc, JD served Iona as its part-time constable. It was JD's patrol car we avoided on midnight adventures. Iona had a ten o'clock curfew.

"We'll take some of these," Billy chirped, waving some paper cotton candy holders. "And some of these." He held up two ears of corn. I replaced the package of straws I had picked up and raised an eyebrow.

"What are you planning?"asked Elva.

"Oh, just a science experiment," Billy lied. "You know, to get a head start on school." I coughed and pretended to straighten the soup cans.

"You're ambitious!" Elva said naïvely. Fifty-seven cents later we exited as fast as we could.

"Science experiment?" I asked. "Are you crazy?"

"You're the one who wanted to smoke. This was the best I could do. Do you want to smoke or not?"

That decided it. We would meet tomorrow behind my garage, hide in the shadows of iniquity, and light up.

Mom loaded me with jobs on the smoking day. I astonished her with my speed. "Can I go play now?" I yelled.

"Kitchen mopped?" she called.

"Yes, Mom."

"Icebox defrosted?"

"All done. Can I go?"

"How about your bedroom?"

"I did my part, but Jeannie didn't do hers."

"Well, you both get in there and finish."

"It's Jeannie's mess!"

I had learned that complaining seldom worked. I grabbed Jeannie by the hand and dragged her to the bedroom where we stashed clothes and toys under our beds. Then I ran to the kitchen, grabbed a box of matches, crashed through the screen door, and hit the ground running.

"Shad, take Jeannie with you," Mom called.

But I sprinted out of sight.

"Wait, Shad!" Jeannie yelled, trying to catch up to me. I feigned deafness. Daniel Boone couldn't have done better in hiding his tracks. I raced around the block to pretend another direction. Then, I doubled back to the garage and waited for Billy.

At two o'clock he slid through the fence boards. Jeannie called for me again, and Billy and I became statues. When we heard the screen door slam we dared to speak, but only in whispers. Billy had the cones and corn. To my astonishment, he pulled a girly magazine from his back pocket. He said he had fished it from the garbage at Jed Bekins Flying Red Horse Gas Station. Billy figured if we were going to smoke we had better do it right.

With the goods spread before us, my hankering for the forbidden began to give way to my conscience. It came like a small voice of warning. What we were about to do, we would not have done at home.

I looked at the magazine, then at Billy. "This isn't right," I said.

Billy shoved an ear of corn in my hand and said to shuck it. "You're not backing out on me now. This was your idea, remember."

Wickedness takes practice, Dad used to say. Billy and I were clumsy sinners.

We bared the kernels of corn of their stubborn, wet silk. Then we realized that no amount of fire would burn the damp stringy stuff. Undaunted, we shoved the silk inside the cotton candy cones and I lifted one to my mouth. Billy lit it.

"Put the small end in your mouth," he said. "Tilt your head back and keep the cone up or you'll get a mouthful of fire."

I obeyed. A burst of flame ignited the dry paper and burned around the wet silk, which fell out. I held the cone between my first and second fingers like the Marlboro Man. If Debby could do it, so could I. I drew a deep breath of smoke into my lungs. It was hot. I coughed and choked and tried to spit the taste from my mouth. I felt my head spin. As I held the smoking cone, the image of a naked woman came under my gaze. She was spread out over two pages. I shut the magazine and my eyes. My brain ached. I squeezed my eyes shut tighter, but I couldn't squeeze out the image. Billy whacked me on the back and I gasped for air.

"This is awful!" I said, eyes tearing.

But before Billy could answer, a voice interrupted. "Shad! What are you doing?" The voice belonged to Jeannie.

"Jeannie! What the *heck* are you doing here!" Except it wasn't "heck" I said. It was Debby's "h" word, and now it belonged to me.

Jeannie began to cry. I wanted to apologize, but the Debby part of me won out. The little voice that had tried to caution me had stopped talking. I felt alone.

I tried to mock. "Oh, look at the baby." I looked at Billy, who was hanging his head. When I turned back, Mom was standing cross-armed next to her sobbing daughter. I didn't have a chance to explain. Mom wagged a finger at me and pulled Jeannie away. Her look of disappointment was a worse punishment than if she'd used a switch.

When they left I turned to Billy and tried to force a smile. But he looked away and scratched the dirt with a stick. Our smokin' and cussin' day was over.

I ate a lonely supper that night. Mostly I chased a green bean around my plate with my fork. My stomach felt knotted and my brain ached. So did my soul. No one spoke to me. I offered to wash the dishes and empty the garbage, but each gesture was met by more silence.

When bedtime came, there was no story, nobody begged me to brush my teeth, I heard no threats to clean my room—just silence. But the little voice had returned. It screamed, "I told you so!"

Summer's sunset turned from orange to black and stars filled Idaho's broad sky. I sat on my bed and gazed out the window at Jeannie sitting alone in the tire swing. At length, I shuffled to my parents' bedroom and knocked.

"Who's there?" came my father's voice.

"Shad. Can I come in?"

When I stepped inside, Dad patted a spot on the bed. I situated myself and fingered the quilted pattern of the bedspread. "I'm sorry," I muttered.

Dad leaned forward and looked me over. "Those are good words if they're real," he said. "At least they're better than the one you used earlier today." I hunched my shoulders. "But it's not so much what you say, it's what you do." I looked up. "The first thing you need to do is make things right with your sister, and then you need to decide how you want to live your life."

He didn't have to say anything else. Mom's eyes were moist and red. I left their room and stepped out into the yard. Jeannie was still in the tire swing. She looked away as I approached. She pretended to play with a stuffed bear she called Missus Muggins. I stood beside her and held one of the ropes of the swing. She didn't move and I took a deep breath. "Today I did some stupid things. The worst was saying a bad word to you. I know it was wrong. I'm sorry."

For a long time, neither of us spoke. I had expected that smokin' and cussin' would make me strong. But I was weak and miserable. I wanted Jeannie to forgive me. But I couldn't forgive myself.

Then she whispered, "Okay." She stood and hugged me. When she let go, she took my arm and I walked her into the house, tucked her and Missus Muggins into bed, and turned off the light. Then I walked outside to sit in the tire swing. I buried my head in my hands and cried through a silent prayer. I promised God I would never again do things against the feelings of my conscience. Peace washed over me and I knew I would be all right.

For years I was reminded of childhood's indiscretion. Without warning, the image of a naked woman would invade my consciousness and haunt my dreams. Only by filling my mind with good thoughts could I finally gain some relief. Over time, the frequency and the intensity of the memory faded. But even today, that experiment with pornography occasionally shoots through my mind without warning and shocks the sensitivities of an older and wiser man.

Making Root Beer

"Ants! Ants!" Mom's voice shot across the kitchen, through the house, out the screen door, and down the steps to where Jeannie and I sat sipping lemonade. "There are ants everywhere!" Mom stomped through the house to find the telephone. She dialed on the black rotary phone. "Is Sam there?" she asked the answerer. "Oh, I see. Will you have him call me? Thanks." Dad would be home late that night. That was good news for the ants.

That summer, Dad found work cleaning construction sites for Zeb's Truss Joist and moving irrigation pipe for farmers. He spent evenings fashioning table legs with a saw and lathe. Mom took in ironing and sewing. The added strain on her crippled leg left her hurting at the end of each day. Jeannie and I took turns massaging the painful area until she could sleep. We knew times were hard. But our parents wrapped us in the blanket of their love, and we forgot we were poor.

Once we begged Dad for ice cream. He hesitated, then reached into his pocket and placed two shiny quarters on the Merc's counter. Only later did we hear our mother's gentle question—how would Dad buy his lunch tomorrow?

Mom paced and fretted about dinner being carried away by ants. Jeannie and I left our lemonade and crouched at the dreaded insects' hole. What we saw was wonderful. A new colony of ants had set up camp in the long crack of our backyard sidewalk.

"Look at these little piles," Jeannie said, pointing at tiny mounds of dirt. Some sleuthing led us to the ants' main trail that beelined to the back porch. Like a disciplined regiment, they had marshaled two single-file columns— one to march to the food, the other to carry it away.

"I'll be right back!" I said. I ran to our bedroom and retrieved a magnifying glass.

"Whoa!" Jeannie exclaimed. "It makes them look huge. What are those things on their heads?"

"Feelers," I responded wisely. "They use their feelers like the antennae on top of our TV." When we had examined them, and poked and prodded them, we decided to fry them with the magnifying glass. We would be entertained and Mom would be rid of the ants.

"This is getting us nowhere," I concluded after an hour. "What we need is a way to kill them all at once." As

I said it out loud, a bud of brilliance sprouted in my mind. "Stay here and watch," I ordered Jeannie, as though the ants might escape if she moved. I ran to the shed where we kept the garden tools. I knew where the gasoline can was.

With can in hand, I ran back to my sister, who stood guard like a sentry. I felt a swell of pride knowing that when Dad was not around I could handle things for Mom like a man. I popped the lid of the gasoline can and let the orange liquid leak down the ants' main hole. I emptied the whole gallon. Jeannie looked at me anxiously. "It's okay," I said. "The gas will drain down to the bottom of their hole. There's no way they can breathe gasoline." When I was certain each opening had been soaked, I set the can aside and Jeannie and I knelt to watch.

Some anomalies of nature are never written into science books. After the initial shock, the resilient ants kept going as if sucking gasoline was just another bump on the road of life.

I rose perplexed. "Stay here and watch," I said. Once more, the ants didn't try to escape. "Don't sniff the fumes!" I shouted. With that command, I marched into the house. I would take care of the ants once and for all.

When I returned with a box of matches, Jeannie yelled, "You're gonna burn them?" I nodded and she ran for the hose. That was wise, I figured. It hadn't crossed my mind that a hose might be needed.

"Stand back!" I barked. She already had. "This will finish them." I cupped my hand around the lit match to shield it from the breeze. The tiny spark became a flame. "Ready?" I looked at Jeannie. She nodded and her knuckles went white around the hose. "Okay," I said, and I tossed the match at the crack in the sidewalk.

The explosion knocked me on my backside. Before I could react, Jeannie vaulted forward and sprayed the sidewalk. She gritted her teeth, shut her eyes, and turned her head away from the spray. I sprang to her side and grabbed the hose. The water made things worse. It only spread the flames more. Suddenly, a fireball jumped to the wooden siding of our house, blistering the paint as it leaped.

"Forget the sidewalk!" Jeannie shouted. "Aim for the side of the house!" The dousing cooled the siding, and after a few moments the fire on the sidewalk burned itself out. The house was drenched. So was Mom, who had come running.

Perhaps Mom made her decision as she stood in the doorway dripping wet; maybe she decided when she surveyed the house I had nearly burned to the ground. Whenever it was, the result was the same. For the next month I spent my mornings scraping the blisters, repainting singed siding, and weeding the vegetable and flower gardens. With enough time for mischief, Mom concluded, I could learn the art of yardwork. We had no more problems with ants that summer.

While I worked in the yard, Jeannie spent her mornings collecting soda pop bottles. Mom's birthday was coming. Jeannie knew Mom adored homemade root beer. When he could afford it, Dad made root beer with dry ice. We children would huddle near to watch Dad stir the delicious bubbly brew. Mom would turn thirty-two in July and Jeannie wanted her to have root beer to celebrate.

J. D. Perkins stocked root beer extract and dry ice. One day Jeannie emptied a mason jar of pennies and nickels on the Merc's counter. Elva accepted her word that she had enough and threw in two peppermint sticks for good measure.

I knew Jeannie's good intentions, but I also knew there was no way a fourth-grader could pull off making root beer. Besides, I figured, here was an opportunity to right the cussing at my sister and square things with Mom for nearly incinerating the house. Jeannie accepted my offer to make the root beer. But we would need Dad's help.

Our plan was this: Dad and Jeannie would kidnap Mom for her birthday, saying they were going to buy her a present. I would stay home, pretend a stomachache, and make the root beer. When they returned, surprise! I couldn't believe Dad bought into my being the brew master. Maybe his motive was to show some faith in a repentant son. In any case, the job fell to me, and by midafternoon of July 2, 1961, the Edna Wane Widener Surprise Root Beer Birthday Party had begun.

Like clockwork, the plan unfolded. Giggling Mom was blindfolded and led from the house. Then I rose from my sickbed. I had an hour before the birthday girl returned.

Making root beer depended on my ability to mimic Dad and remember the steps. "First," I thought, "I need a big pot." The thought of sipping the bubbly, brown beverage caused my mouth to water.

I read the directions: "Pour five gallons of water into a large container and add the bottle of extract."

"Never mind five gallons," I thought, "this is my mother's birthday. I'll make ten gallons!" Of course, I had no idea what a ten-gallon container looked like. The largest pot I could find was the one Mom used for bottling fruit. I eyeballed a gallon of milk and tried to imagine ten of them. "Close enough," I concluded.

I could find only a cereal bowl to fill the pot with water. The minutes flew faster than the pot filled. I was running out of time! Fifty minutes had elapsed when I removed the cap from the bottle of root beer extract and emptied its contents into the water. The thick fluid snaked to the bottom of the pot, and I stirred the mixture with a big wooden spoon.

"Add one pound of sugar for each gallon of water," the label read.

I knew the drawer where Mom kept the sugar. I had helped myself to a spoonful now and then. My anxiety pulsed with every tick of the grandfather clock. I hurried to the sugar drawer. Empty! Debby's cuss word flitted across my mind.

I began rummaging through adjacent drawers. "Sugar! Sugar!" I mumbled, as if saying it would make it appear. I reached for the cupboard. Maybe Mom had found a new place to store it. Then I stumbled onto an alternative: brown sugar. For just a moment I considered that this might not work. But urgency blocked reason. "Sugar's sugar," I thought. I grabbed all three packages, dumped them in, and stirred the pot until the ingredients turned a pleasant brown. Then I crushed the block of dry ice with a hammer and piled the pieces into the tub.

Immediately a reaction erupted that I could not stop. The dry ice roused the water to a quick boil. Clouds of carbonation billowed from the pot, eclipsing my vision. I groped for the back of a chair. When the fog thinned, I saw exploding bubbles heaving root beer all over Mom's kitchen. I tried to stay ahead of the mess by throwing towels around the tub. When the boiling slowed, I gathered the soaked towels and threw them into a corner. Then I knelt, blew aside the mist, and dipped my cup to test it.

I was not prepared for what passed over my tongue. One sip was all I could endure. I stepped back, crouched on my haunches, and stared at the concoction. It seemed to scorn me with every bursting bubble. Not one idea entered my mind that could transform the ten gallons of swill to root beer.

The clock chimed mournfully. I still squatted, defeated. The time for Mom's party had come and gone. The kitchen looked as if a bomb had exploded. Brown liquid covered the once-white floor. Drenched towels were piled in a corner looking like drowned rats. Brown sugar was stuck to everything.

Another hour passed without my family's return. For that hour I cleaned, mopped, shined, and dried. Mom shouldn't have to come home to two disasters on her birthday, I thought. Another thirty minutes passed. I stood alone in the middle of a clean kitchen. I couldn't imagine what had delayed them. I decided to wash out the root beer-soaked towels. Then I realized I was hungry.

Peanut butter and grape jelly were my best effort at a meal. When I sat down to my plate, I felt overwhelming remorse—not for the peanut butter sandwich, but for Jeannie's surprise. I knew how long she had scouted soda pop bottles. I had no idea how many she had pawned before she had earned enough to buy the root beer extract.

I patted the peanut butter sandwich shut and purple goo oozed out from its sides. I decided I would give thanks for it as I had been taught, even though I didn't feel very thankful.

"Heavenly Father," I began my silent prayer in rote, "I thank thee for this food and ask thee to bless it. . . ." Then I paused a moment, wondering if what I wanted to ask was appropriate. "I feel terrible about ruining Jeannie's little bottle of root beer extract. If there's anything you can do, I sure would appreciate it. Amen."

I doubted that my half-hearted prayer had escaped the ceiling. I imagined my words caught somewhere in the blades of the ceiling fan.

I finished my sandwich and retired to the front room to watch westerns on television. But before the drovers could round up the dogies, the stress and the peanut butter sandwich took their toll, and I fell asleep in the middle of a five-man gunfight. I awoke to the sound of gleeful voices in the kitchen. My mother's was the happiest and loudest.

"Root beer! Oh, you shouldn't have," she exclaimed. "Give me a cup!"

"We'll all have one," said Dad. "A toast!"

"A toast," echoed Jeannie.

By that time, I had bounced to my feet and was racing to the kitchen to stop a tragedy. But when I arrived all three were gulping root beer as if it were going out of style.

"Shad!" squealed Mom when she saw me. "Sorry we're late. We had a flat tire. But this root beer was worth it. It's the best I've ever tasted!"

"The best," said Jeannie.

"It's settled, then," said Dad, lifting his mug in the air. "Shad is hereby dubbed the official Widener Family Root Beer Meister."

I wanted to slug my arm to see if I was dreaming. The thought crossed my mind that maybe they were teasing me. But I dismissed it, recalling the awful taste and knowing that none of them could act that well.

Dad continued, "Let's have another toast to the most beautiful mother in the world, to her wonderful daughter who made this occasion possible, to her marvelous son whose talents we are just beginning to discover, and to her handsome husband who keeps her in the lap of luxury."

I eyed the root beer and lifted it to my lips. I allowed a few drops to slide over my tongue. It was delicious! I sampled it again and again. It was wonderful.

"Oh, Shad," Jeannie gushed, "you're the best!"

I looked at Mom and Dad, who nodded.

"Well," I said, "I had some help."

No one knew what I meant. No one cared. We laughed and sang and gulped root beer into the night. The Edna Wane Widener Surprise Root Beer Birthday Party was a roaring success. And because I had brewed so much, we drank root beer at every meal—even breakfast—for the next week.

I have never understood the miracle of the root beer. But long ago I decided that if water could be turned into wine by the simple word of God, perhaps a young boy's prayer over root beer could make it taste better. Or maybe God has a sense of humor. That's how I choose to picture him. In any case, I have since appreciated that he listens to every prayer—even those over peanut butter sandwiches and bad root beer.

What Would
John Wayne Do?

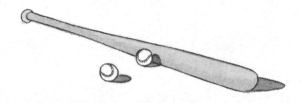

Jeannie and I sat on the porch comparing big toes sticking out the ends of our sneakers. The sides of our shoes were frayed and holey, and the sole of mine flapped freely. Dad had called us to a family council to explain that our finances had worsened. I had come to anticipate the serious nature of such councils since an earlier one had announced our move from Ucon to Iona. That summer, Jeannie and I became proficient at repairing our shoes with duct tape.

Poorer than we, however, were the strange Shimmels. August brought Sheila from her house, which lay in the shadows where the bats flew. She stood tall and plump, easily making two of me. Her dark hair was stringy and wild. A hint of facial hair suggested sideburns and a mustache. Acne dotted her chin and nose. She was two years my senior. Her appearance piqued the curiosity of local boys and girls.

Within days of her emerging, a joke about Sheila's having fleas spread like wildfire through town. It started in mocking jest but was quickly believed. Soon the worst thing someone could get was Sheila's fleas. Once contaminated, it might take an hour, a day, or even longer to get rid of them.

We played the game like this: Someone scourged with Sheila's fleas would pretend to hold them in his fist. If that person could get close to another and touch him, the fleas were transferred, and "the giver" would yell, "You've got Sheila's fleas!" Then the newly cured would run like the devil so the fleas couldn't be given back. Worse than the fleas, the now-contaminated became "It." If one were slow, like fat Tommy Harrigan, one could be "It" for a long time. Tommy held the record at three days, six hours, and forty-seven minutes.

I played the game. Jeannie wouldn't. I liked the fun. I couldn't see the hurt.

Summer brought other games. Billy had earned the coveted position of first base on our baseball team. Jeannie wanted to be on the team, but we wouldn't let her, although she could bat and throw better than most boys on the team. She targeted Cotton Langford's right-field position.

"Hey, batter, batter, batter," Jeannie yelled at Cotton, who couldn't swing worth beans.

"Shut up, you creep!" he hollered. "Shad, can't you make her be quiet?"

I tried to put my hand over Jeannie's mouth, but she pushed it away. "Your mother wears army boots!" she screamed. Cotton took strike two.

"I'm warning you, Widener!" he yelled.

"Be quiet, Jeannie!" I shushed her. But she gave me no heed.

"Hey, pitch," Jeannie gibed through cupped hands, "maybe you should throw it underhand."

I saw Cotton's face grow red. He gritted his teeth and stared steely-eyed at the pitcher. The white sphere left the pitcher's hand with lightning speed. Cotton's swing reverberated over the baseball field, sending him staggering backwards.

"Strike three!"

Jeannie rolled on her stomach laughing. I tried to nudge her as Cotton Langford stepped toward her, steaming.

"Maybe you could do better!" he said, shoving his bat at her.

"With my eyes closed," she bragged, suddenly serious.

"I dare you," said Cotton. "I double dare . . . no, I *triple* dare you!"

The entire team gasped.

"Jeannie," I whispered, "maybe it's time to go home."

Jeannie stood, as though she hadn't heard me. I knew there would be trouble. Boys cut each other slack, but challenged by a girl, they would try harder than ever.

Jeannie rubbed her hands in the dirt, spit into them, and wiped them on her pants. Then she stepped to the batter's box and beat her bat on the plate. She assumed the batter's position, gripping the bat an inch from the handle.

"Show her no mercy!" an outfielder shouted.

"Stuff it down her throat!" barked Cotton.

Soon the entire team had joined in. Jeannie stood stoic, undistracted. Her eyes froze on the pitcher. She dug her toe into the earth and tightened her grip on the bat. The pitcher planted his foot and began his windup. With a loud grunt, he let sail a powerful pitch that spun crazily toward Jeannie. I saw her muscles tense and explode as she swung her bat. The solid crack told all in earshot that something wonderful had happened.

Two positions opened in the lineup after Jeannie's hit: the first when she slid into second base and took out Robby Barton, the second when Cotton Langford was demoted to batboy. Jeannie was given Cotton's right field position. I had to prove myself since local baseball circles remembered that Debby had labeled my throw as a girl's.

Our first day of practice was memorable. Spence Christiansen, the shortstop, noticed that Jeannie's shoes were wrapped in tape and made a laughable point about them. He shut up when Jeannie kicked dirt on him and called him a fat goose. But the following practice Billy showed up with his shoes duct-taped, and a fad began. Over night, duct-taped sneakers were cool. They became the signature look for our team, since none of us could afford uniforms.

There was more to learn about baseball than I had imagined. For example, I discovered the hard way that areas of the baseball field had been staked out by Debby as his territory. These areas were not marked, but they were known and avoided by Iona boys. Debby's ownership had never been challenged until that Tuesday morning. I laced my fingers through the wire webbing of his backstop. Someone had forgotten to warn me.

"Get your hands off our backstop!" I turned to see Jeepers, who stood front-center of Debby's band—Debby in the middle.

"Your backstop?" I swallowed hard.

Jeepers didn't answer, but Debby did. He stepped forward and hurled a knuckled fist into my stomach. I doubled over and gasped for air. Ball practice came to a standstill. Not one teammate stepped forward to help me. Debby backed them up with a glare, then walked away, his company following.

"Hey, buzzard breath!" Jeannie shouted. She came running in from right field. She burst into the middle of the mob, pushing and shoving until she stood toe to toe with Debby. "You're not so tough!" she yelled, and kicked him in the shin.

Debby grabbed his leg and Billy rushed to pull her away. "You better do something with her or she'll be dog meat!" Debby bellowed as he hobbled away.

I fell to the ground and clutched my middle. My lungs burned. Jeannie and the team ran to me.

"Roll him on his back and push his knees to his chest!" Spence cried. His command helped, for soon I could breathe and my stomach relaxed. When I sat up I wiped my eyes and the team allowed me a few moments alone. Practice ended.

From then on, I avoided *Debby's* backstop. But Debby and his gang stalked the ball field. Our team maintained a respectful distance. Often I glanced in Debby's direction. He was always staring at me. Sometimes he would roll up his sleeves and flex his biceps. Then his group would light up cigarettes and jeer. It was enough to frighten the bravest of Iona.

One Thursday, Debby found me on the ball field and slugged the air out of me just for *looking* at his backstop. Jeannie tried to fight him, but once more she was held by Billy and others. When Debby punched me on Friday for showing up, fear swept through the team and some suggested I should quit. I considered it. Baseball wasn't fun anymore. I no longer rose each morning to the smell of leather and the feel of dirt. I had to sneak to the ball field and surround myself with my teammates.

That Saturday looms as one of the most humiliating days of my life.

It had begun like any other morning that week— sneaking to the ballpark, hiding in shadows. I had decided to go early to avoid trouble. Jeannie was eating breakfast when I left. Midway to the ballpark, I caught a glimpse of Jeepers darting behind a tree. Since the first time I'd met him, I didn't like him. That he was alone was alarming, for where Jeepers was, Debby couldn't be far away. So, when Jeepers jumped at me from behind a mulberry bush, I should have known better than to confront him.

"Get out of my way, pipsqueak!" I hollered.

"Say 'pleeease,'" he taunted.

"Drop dead!" I tried to walk around him.

Jeepers stepped into my path. "You didn't say 'please.'"

"You see Hammond's barn?" I said, gesturing.

"Yeah?"

"Make sure you get a good run when you jump off the top!" I shouted, pushing him hard out of the way.

When Jeepers hit the ground several figures led by one with bulging biceps emerged from behind the bush. I froze. I was surrounded. Debby soothed his little companion. "Here," he said, "let me help you up." Debby lifted Jeepers to his feet and brushed him off. "Now, who would hurt a nice little fellow like you?"

Jeepers faked a snivel and pointed an accusing finger.

"So," said Debby, turning to me, "you're the bully who beats up little kids?"

"N-n-no! It was an accident. I'm sorry!"

But no one wanted an apology.

"What do we do with bullies?" Debby asked his pack.

"Get a rope!" cried one.

"Make him walk the plank!" yelled another.

"Cement boots!"

"Bamboo under his fingernails!"

"Great ideas," Debby said. "But Jeepers should get to choose."

I knew I was dead when Jeepers materialized with a BB gun and pointed it at my head. Only a boy who has coveted a BB gun and has been warned by parents of its maiming ability can appreciate the fear that sliced through my body. I began to shake. One twitch of his trigger finger and I would be playing ball in the big diamond in the sky.

"On your knees!" Jeepers shouted. Debby forced me to the ground.

"Okay! Okay!" I said. "Don't shoot!"

I began to cry when Jeepers commanded me to crawl around on all fours, barking like Lassie. The mob laughed and heckled, each aiming a kick at my rear end. Next came dancing like a ballerina, followed by singing "Rudolph, the Red-Nosed Reindeer" while standing on my head.

I was crying hard when Jeepers said to reach for the sky and march. I knew I was headed for my execution. With my back turned, I didn't notice Debby and the others disappear. I was left to be paraded by Jeepers. I didn't dare turn. Jeepers marched me, and Debby and friends hid behind trees and watched. I didn't know Jeepers had also discarded the BB gun and held only a stick to my back. What a scene it must have been—Jeepers marching me up and down Main Street with a stick, as I held my hands high, bawling and begging for mercy.

Then I heard hooting. I turned and found myself alone. Jeepers and all the boys catcalled and pointed at me from across the street. Elva Perkins stood at the entrance of the Merc. Maudy Tyler peered from behind curtains of her front room window.

Jeannie rushed to see the cause of the commotion. I lowered my hands, wiped my eyes, and ran past her into the house. Mom found me. I guessed Jeannie had turned me in, or Maudy had phoned her. My public display of cowardice was now a topic. Mom sat on the davenport beside me. Jeannie sat in a corner.

"I'm not going to ever play baseball again," I whimpered. "Why did we ever move here? I want to go back to Ucon."

Mom drew my head into her lap and I cried big tears. She ran her fingers through my hair and rocked me. "I suppose there are bullies everywhere who see themselves as big by tormenting younger and smaller people. Ucon has them, too. I expect every town does. It's not where you live, but how you live."

I looked up.

"I'd like to run away from some of my problems," she said. "So would your dad. But every day we have to get up and face life. We hope it isn't always this hard. I have to believe that if we keep trying, the hard times will end."

"You're big, though," I said. "I get beat up every day."

"Big doesn't matter," she said. "There's always someone who will hurt you if you let them." She paused then. "Shad? Why do you let it happen?"

"I have no choice."

"You always have a choice. If you have tried the peaceful way and it doesn't work, you don't have to take a beating—protect yourself. Fight back!"

I couldn't believe this was my mom talking. If ever there was a person who exemplified turning the other cheek, it was Mom. Fight back?

"I'd get killed!" I protested.

"Fear is the worst death of all," she said. "You must face your problems bravely, not on your knees. Besides," she continued, "you're not going to die—you are going to be free."

"I'm going to be beaten to a bloody pulp!"

"Better a bloody pulp than a frightened child." Her firm voice cut through my cowardice. "Remember when you were four and you had nightmares every night? You were convinced there was a monster in your closet."

I remembered.

"How did you get over those fears?"

"Every night you made me open the closet until I could chase the monster from my mind."

"Chase the monster away, Shad! It's only a monster if you let it be. What would John Wayne do?" I didn't even know she knew who John Wayne was. She hugged me and I pulled away. She wiped her eyes and pointed me toward the door. I later learned that when I left the house she fell on her knees, wept, and begged for the safety of her son.

An impending showdown brings determination or fear. I'd seen John Wayne movies and I knew. As I walked down

Main Street seeking Debby, I felt a surge. I set my jaw.

"Debby, you freak-faced pile of moose droppings," I shouted, "I'm looking for you!" I was careful not to step back into cussing. I had only to yell it once. Debby slid from the shadows, chewing the butt of a cigarette. His gang followed.

"You want somethin'?"

"I'm here to have it out, once and for all," I said, making a fist and hitting the cup of my hand. Jeepers and another stepped toward me, but I moved them back with a look.

"This pleasure's all mine," Debby sneered, as he rolled up his sleeves and exposed his muscles.

A bolt of fear shot through me.

I raised my fists like a boxer's. Debby laughed. I danced around, then threw a wild punch at Debby's chin. He ducked and countered with a strike to my eye. The next thing I knew I was sitting on my backside in the dirt. I staggered to my feet and swung again. Once more, Debby dodged and landed a hard left to my nose. Blood spurted everywhere. Again, I rose to my feet. I hadn't time to raise my fists when I was knocked to the ground with an uppercut to my jaw.

"It's over," Debby yelled. "Stay down."

I didn't obey. I teetered to my feet and beckoned him to continue. He eyed me with a puzzled look. When he came close I threw my best punch. He caught it as though one-handing a baseball. Then he slugged me hard on the chin. For the fourth time I fell.

"Stay down!" he ordered.

I wiped the blood from my face and tried to stand, but my legs wouldn't hold me.

"It's over!" Debby shouted.

I tried to rise, but fell back into the dirt. The boys of Debby's gang began to cheer, but he told them to be quiet. Then Debby reached down, grabbed me by the forearm and pulled me to my feet. "You're all right," he said. Then he brushed me off, stepped aside, and the entire group — even open-mouthed Jeepers—came forward and patted me on the back.

In a moment I was standing alone. My nose had stopped bleeding, but I wished it hadn't. I wanted everyone to see it. My eye had swollen shut and I could hardly open my mouth, but strangely, I couldn't feel them. I knew what John Wayne would do: When life hurt him, he would pick himself up, brush himself off, wipe away the blood, and ride off tall in the saddle.

I walked home proud. When I passed Sheila Shimmel's house I saw movement behind the curtains. She had been watching. I stopped and surveyed the Shimmel home. I could see nothing that suggested insanity, only poverty. I saw a wood stack, and expected that was their only source of heat. I noticed the curled shingles that would not withstand another Idaho winter. The chipped paint told of long years of disrepair. My pride turned to shame. There are many ways to bloody a weaker person. I tried to justify my actions, but it did no good. The honest part of me knew I had acted no better to Sheila than Debby had to me.

Sheila Has Fleas

SEPTEMBER BROUGHT PROMISE of harvest, sleeping indoors, school's beginning, and Heck Markham.

Hector Markham knew Dad's woodworking skills and had an idea that there was money to be made in contract carpentry. Mr. Markham was a man known for his dubious ethics. His self-described business of "undefined and varying interests" provided him a handsome living. Dad said Heck would chase a dollar wherever it could be found. We knew Mr. Markham because he attended our church. He prayed and sang with righteous fervor and dominated Sunday School discussions. When Mr. Markham offered Dad $4,000 to build two hundred wooden chairs, Dad was more than suspicious. He told Mr. Markham thanks, the proposal would be considered.

Mom's laundry business provided Jeannie and me with crayons, paper, pencils, India ink, and black pens. Jeannie sold soda pop bottles for jacks and hair ribbons. I earned marble money by trapping gophers with Billy—twenty-five cents for each tail sold to the county. Shrewd trading coupled with a steady shooter thumb expanded my bag of cat's-eyes to five clearies, a steely, and two agates. The little cache became the foundation of my marble empire.

In September I stepped into Mrs. Campbell's sixth-grade classroom. It was filled with wooden lift-top desks, evenly spaced on runners. The front wall was covered by a blackboard bordered by samples of cursive letters of the alphabet. Its cleaning by the unruly became a focal point of punishment. I took my turn tidying it. The classroom's side walls sported corkboards of varying sizes, meant to display sixth-grade art, prize-winning poetry, and worthy essays. On the right side of the classroom, Mrs. Campbell sat at her desk. It was positioned so that it guarded the closet where the tetherballs and basketballs were locked.

As custom demanded, Iona Elementary students, on the first day of school, rushed into their new classrooms and staked claims to the desks of their choice. This practice was allowed until teachers developed seating charts. A pretty pink notebook lay on a desk at the front of Mrs. Campbell's classroom. I knew by the name etched on the cover where Rebecca Reeder would sit.

The Reeder family was longtime Iona stock, descended from the early pioneers. Rebecca—nicknamed Rebe—was Ralph and Georgia Reeder's youngest and most beautiful daughter. I had first seen her in the summer playing "Ollie, Ollie Oxen Free" with shapeless girls with knobby knees. From that moment, I had planned for this day. Sitting next to Rebe became my obsession.

I seized the desk behind Rebe's. Here, seated behind her, I would be inspired all day, I thought. Here, her strawberry-colored ponytail would dance on my desktop. Here, I could watch her all I wanted without her knowing.

I had entered unfamiliar territory. In July I had admired Libby Berry's big brown eyes. But I had stopped before mentioning Libby or her eyes to Billy or any other Iona boys. In 1961, girls were either tolerated or ignored. By 1962, that would change forever.

When I saw Rebe enter the room, something awoke within me like a shout of rejoicing. I stood when Rebe walked toward her desk.

"Sit down, Mr. Widener!" said Mrs. Campbell. An explosion of laughter burst from the class. I sat and hid my hot face. Rebe turned and glanced at me, then flipped her strawberry-blond hair with her hand. I was smitten. Suddenly, a belated laugh came from the back of the room. Sheila Shimmel had decided to join in the gaiety. I melted into my seat. My resolve to try and understand Sheila gave way to embarrassment. Things were about to get worse.

"Mr. Widener, trade seats with Mr. Bitner," Mrs. Campbell said, without raising her eyes from her seating chart.

Leon Bitner cheerfully moved forward to the envied desk behind Rebe. He had vacated the seat at the rear of the room next to Sheila. What had promised to be the best year of my life was beginning as a nightmare. What was worse, partnering off was Mrs. Campbell's favorite mode of drilling lessons. She also used it to help slower students improve with the assistance of brighter ones. From that day forward, I was condemned to work with Sheila Shimmel. I would be assigned to coach her in reading and math.

When the class split into groups, Leon sat with Rebe and I sat with Sheila. When recess came, Leon and Rebe's group departed first, and Sheila's and mine exited last. Lunchtime was no better. When Rebe chose Leon for her kickball team, I thought my life was over.

Then Sheila's fleas resurfaced. Because I sat next to her, I spent every recess ridding myself of them. Sheila hadn't the mental capacity to know she was the butt of a joke. For her, any attention was welcome, and she laughed as we dodged her fleas.

When the joke grew old, other contamination possibilities were invented. It started when someone decided that Sheila's fleas could be transferred by drinking after her at the water fountain. At break time, everyone would jockey for position so that Sheila would have to drink last. In the playground, we avoided stepping where Sheila had stepped. Monkey bars were shunned after she had used them.

I pretended interest but only joined in when the fleas fell on me. Otherwise, my whole attention was dedicated to a blue-eyed strawberry blonde with dimples. But I was certain she had no interest in me.

One morning I awakened to Jeannie screaming and pointing at my face. "You've got the gravies, the gravies! You've got to get shots in your belly button! You're going to die!" Jeannie's class had been learning about rabid dogs. The lesson had made an impression on her, for when she saw the big red pimple on my chin she knew I was infected.

I ran to the bathroom and looked in the mirror. Sure enough, a huge red blemish had blossomed on my chin. I could forget Rebe, the giant scarlet zit had decided that.

"Toad! Freak! Repulsive pig!" I bellowed from the bathroom. Mom came running.

"Shad? Are you all right?" She pounded on the door.

"I'm fine."

"Let me in!"

"I'm okay. I'll be out in a while."

"Right now, young man!"

Reluctantly, I released the lock and cracked open the door. I held a washcloth over my chin where I had dug and squeezed it. Mom reached out to remove the washcloth and I retreated.

"Hold still," she said. She removed the washcloth from my chin, looked relieved, and smiled. I stared at the floor.

"It's just a pimple," she said.

"It's the gravies!" yelled Jeannie.

"It's the ugliest thing I've ever seen," I replied.

"Nonsense," said Mom. "Both of you stop being dramatic. All boys and girls get them. It means you are growing up." Then she sat me down and dabbed a little makeup on my chin. "Just keep your face washed and don't worry about it. That will only make things worse."

"But I can't go to school looking like this."

"You'll have to get shots in your belly button!" Jeannie said.

Mom scolded her daughter and turned back to me. "Then you'll miss a lot of school over the next few years. If you're worried about what Billy and the other boys will say—don't. They'll get pimples, too, if they haven't already."

"It's not Billy I'm worried about." I bit my tongue.

Mom hesitated. "Do you want to tell me?"

"No." But I did want to tell her. I had to tell somebody. I had carried the burden of my love for Rebe for too long.

"Is it a girl?"

"No!" I lied.

"I see," she said. "And you're sure you don't want to talk?"

I shook my head.

"I'll bet I know who it is," shouted Jeannie. "I've seen the notes you hide under your mattress."

"Be quiet, Jeannie!" I yelled. "Mom, tell her to stop."

Jeannie paid me no mind. "It's Rebe!"

"Rebecca Reeder?" Mom exclaimed. Suddenly, Mom and Jeannie were cackling like two hens over a juicy worm.

"She's a doll!" said Mom. Then she turned to me. "This *is* serious."

I looked at her. "Now you know why I can't go to school like this. She'll hate me." I looked at my duct-taped shoes and touched my patched jeans. I had never complained before, but my pride won out. "I look like something out of a horror show!"

Jeannie elbowed me. "Shad! Take it back!" But it was too late. I could see the hurt in Mom's face. I knew she and Dad were doing all they could to provide clothes and food, and the blemish wasn't her fault.

Mom took my hand and led me to the kitchen, where she had prepared breakfast. "Eat," she said, "and we'll talk."

Then Mom hurried Jeannie off to school.

"I wanna stay!" Jeannie complained.

"No!"

Jeannie kicked at some rocks as she left the house.

When Mom returned to the kitchen, I told her I was sorry. She roughed up my hair and smiled.

"Mom?"

"Yes?"

"Were you ever in love before you met Dad?"

She thought for a moment, then said, "Oh, I thought I was once or twice, but it was just indigestion." I could see she thought it was funny. I forced a polite laugh. She went to the living room and returned with a photo album. "Here's my class picture when I was your age. That's me, the buck-toothed one with the thick glasses and the leg braces." She pointed to a skinny girl. I could imagine hearing her classmates mocking and teasing her. "That's Frank Simmons," she said, pointing at a picture of a dark-haired boy. "Oh, he was handsome. I had such a crush. I cried so many tears because he loved Ellen May." Mom thumbed through the pictures. "Here's Ray Jerrott and me at a school party. He was fun and loved to dance. But I couldn't with my bad leg, so that relationship didn't last long."

"So what was different when you met Dad?"

"He loved Mendelssohn," she replied.

"I don't understand."

"Wait here." She cleared the table and brought her record player from the closet. "Listen to this," she whispered. I opened my mouth but she motioned for me to be quiet. Then, when she had placed the needle, she leaned back in her chair.

Her selection was one she had urged me to learn to appreciate. I had cringed each time I tried. Today I would be Mom's captive. For thirty minutes she taught me the genius of Felix Mendelssohn's "Violin Concerto in E Minor."

Mom explained the instrumentation, the transitions, and the skill the composer displayed. "Listen," she said, when the first movement ended. "Mendelssohn hated noise at concerts. He despised coughing and the moving of chairs. So, without a break, he ran the first movement into the second, using only the single tone of an oboe."

A new movement began. This was her favorite.

I was amazed at my mother's knowledge of the music and the man. She not only knew the composition but she could identify every instrument and knew how Mendelssohn incorporated it for effect. She closed her eyes and pretended to be the conductor. Later, when the violin soared above the orchestra, she lifted an invisible instrument to her chin and imitated the performer. Finally, when the concerto ended, she lifted the needle from the record and slipped it into its sleeve. "Let me tell you the story of the Mendelssohn family," she said. That day my education was in the hands of my mother.

Mom seemed to look past the ceiling and began. "Felix Mendelssohn's grandfather, Moses, was reared in the Jewish ghetto of Dessau in Germany. At fourteen, he departed and walked eighty miles to Berlin. The only entrance for Jews was called Rosenthaler Gate. When he arrived, the watchman at the gate asked his name and why he had come.

"'I am Moses,' he declared, 'and I have come to learn.' The watchman swung open the gate and cried, 'Go, Moses, for the sea has opened before you!'

"I doubt that history has seen youths so determined to learn. Moses would not be bound by the ghetto wall that surrounded Dessau, cutting him off from Europe's culture. Despite the fact that he was a Jew, born small and hump-backed, and spoke with a stammer, Moses was irrepressible and devoted his life to reducing the ghetto's wall to rubble. He first mastered the German language, then its literature. He studied Christianity and taught himself Latin. He learned English, French, and geometry—all this without attending a university.

"Soon, the reputation of his intellect and accomplishments spread throughout the Jewish community in Berlin.

By the age of thirty-three he was known as a philosopher, thinker, and writer. He had a significant following of faithful and learned friends. In fact, he had everything a man could want except for what he wanted most—a wife and family.

"His friends introduced him to young ladies, but of those introductions none resulted in marriage. He knew why. His most attractive asset was his mind. Otherwise, his small distorted body was a terrible barrier. He had not met a young woman who could look past it. Then it was arranged that Moses would meet Fromet Gugenheim. Fromet's father, an enthusiastic follower of Moses, had planned the meeting in Hamburg, Germany. Moses was totally taken with her. Although she was neither educated nor significantly lovely, she had deep-blue eyes and beautiful dark hair. Moses later confided that he was an 'infatuated fool.'

"On the other hand, when Fromet first saw Moses she burst into tears. Her father had spoken only of his character and his mind. The sight of his stunted, misshapen figure reduced her to sobs. Moses knew why. He invited her to spend a moment alone with him in the garden. After they had walked awhile Fromet realized that she didn't need to be frightened. Finally he asked her directly, 'Is it my hump?' He turned slightly to profile the deformity. His honesty encouraged hers. She nodded. He led her to a bench.

"'Let me tell you a story, then,' he said, 'which I have never before told to any person. When a Jewish child is about to be born, a proclamation is made in heaven of the name of the person that child is to one day marry. Before I was born, my future wife was also named, and it was said that she would be humpbacked. 'O God,' I prayed, 'a deformed girl will become embittered and unhappy. Let me have the humpback, and make the maiden flawless and beautiful.'

"Fromet then saw in Moses enough love and goodness to hide any imperfection. They were married that year."

After Mom finished the story she reached across the table and took my hands. "Your dad introduced me to Felix Mendelssohn's music on our first date. We have enjoyed listening to it ever since." I looked into her eyes for understanding. "Shad," she said, "real love covers any shortcoming. That's the kind of love your dad and I have for each other. He looks past my imperfections and I look past his. If Rebe is worth loving, she won't care what you look like or how you dress. She will see past the surface, deep down into your soul where everything is beautiful—just like I do."

"Mom?" I asked, "when did you know you were in love with Dad?"

"When I knew I would give everything I had for him." She squeezed a paper into my hand and left. It read:

> You love to the level of your sacrifice.
> You serve to the level of your love.

She returned, carrying a bundle of ironing. The money she would earn would buy her children lunches for a week.

My blemish had turned a comfortable pink by the next morning. Jeannie had stopped staring at my navel. No one said anything about the pimple. In fact, I noticed other blossoming faces. Rebe's was not among them. Her cream-colored skin was pure. My love for her heightened, but she still hadn't noticed me.

Ten-fifteen brought break time. Pushing and shoving at the water fountain always drew a crowd. Inevitably someone got sprayed. Everyone knew the drinking and spraying had to happen before Sheila got in line.

One day an extraordinary thing happened: Sheila managed to get to the water fountain first. Everyone stared and gathered around her. When she finished she looked up as if she didn't know exactly how to react to all the attention. No one knew what to do. So we all just stood there gaping. Then Thurston Haddock pushed Therrill Lewis toward the fountain. "Take a drink," he said laughing, "and get a mouthful of fleas."

That started the joking and pushing. Soon the whole circle joined in. Sheila was caught in the middle. I stood outside the crowd and searched for Rebe, thinking maybe I would say "Hi" or something clever.

Suddenly I saw my sister Jeannie push open the girls' lavatory door. When she saw Sheila's tormentors, a scowl crossed her face and she clenched her fists. I couldn't get to her fast enough. I knew what was about to happen.

"Get out of my way!" she hollered. She marched toward the circle and parted it. Thurston Haddock took a step toward her, but Jeannie shoved him back. Then she stepped to Sheila's side and glared at the crowd. Everyone quieted. Jeannie looked at Sheila and turned to the water fountain. We held our breath. Then Jeannie took a long drink.

I heard gasps. Jeannie hadn't finished. She reached out to Sheila's shoulder, grabbed a handful of imaginary fleas, and slapped them on herself.

Someone said, "Now you've got Sheila's fleas forever!"

"That's right!" another agreed. "You'll never get rid of them."

The circle closed and tightened and, for the first time, Jeannie looked frightened. She and Sheila moved back as the group closed in, taunting them.

I forced my way through the mob and came to where Jeannie and Sheila stood quailing. Then I took a deep breath, stretched out my hand, took the fleas from Jeannie, and slapped them on my chest. No one snickered, nobody said I was infected or crazy. Heads dropped, and slowly the group returned to class. Soon, Jeannie, Sheila, and I were alone—except for Rebe Reeder, who had left the group and come to us.

Jeannie smiled at her, then at Sheila, then at me. Then the bell rang and she ran to class. Rebe shot me a big smile. "Will you walk me home today?" she said.

I tried to say "Uh-huh," but it got caught in my throat. I just nodded.

Then Rebe turned to Sheila, took her hand, and said, "Come with me." And she led her back to class.

Sheila's fleas had died forever, and we gained a friend. Thereafter, acceptance of our peculiar classmate became *cool*. By the end of sixth grade, Sheila was elected honorary class president. As for Rebe, she grew more lovely with each passing day and never had a pimple. We became great friends. I was Moses Mendelssohn and she was my Fromet. And from that distant beginning, a tiny seed sprouted that blossomed into something I would give everything I had or was to own.

A Cry in the Dark

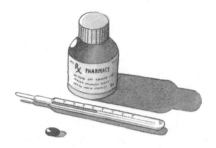

OCTOBER'S CHILL TURNED LEAVES red and orange. When they blanketed the yard of the house, Jeannie and I raked them into huge piles and plunged into them as if they were goose-down mattresses.

October sent us rummaging through boxes of winter clothing for coats that had grown too small.

October afternoons sent us to neighbors' trees and gardens to pick ripe fruits and vegetables. Those gracious invitations were godsends.

October days warmed Mom's kitchen, where she bottled the fruits and vegetables for another long Idaho winter.

October found our family's financial situation worse than ever—no more irrigation pipe; scant carpentry work.

October brought a strep epidemic that crippled southeastern Idaho and nearly closed our school.

I was the first Widener infected. I awoke one morning with a blazing sore throat and a crushing headache. I chilled and ached, then sweated, and had to be sponged with rubbing alcohol. When my situation did not improve, my parents wrapped me against the autumn chill and drove me to the doctor in Idaho Falls.

Dr. Callahan's office occupied the underground level of a medical building covered in green ivy. As we entered, the antiseptic smell made my stomach turn, reminding it of previous visits. The room was dim and pale green. The nurses' desk was where we signed up and checked in our dignity. In the waiting area, sick children played with each other's toys, and parents thumbed through magazines. I watched tropical fish swim in a big aquarium.

Soon a tall nurse with a white Florence Nightingale cap on her head called my name. My parents and I followed her to an examination room. Jeannie was told to stay and watch the fish. I sat on a steel table and was told to disrobe. The nurse returned, dipped a cold thermometer in alcohol, and stuck it in my mouth. I held it under my tongue while she checked my blood pressure. When she had scribbled the results, she left, saying Dr. Callahan would come soon.

I tried to relax. On the wall hung a Norman Rockwell print depicting a happy, bare-bottomed baby with a stern-faced doctor looming behind it, holding a huge needle. The infant's parents shrank in the corner, hiding their faces.

Dr. Callahan entered wearing a round mirror on his head. He washed his hands and then pondered my chart.

"Now, what brings us here today?" he asked. I knew "us" meant me.

"We have a sore throat," I said.

He laughed politely, then stuck a wooden stick down my throat and pressed it against my tongue. "Uh-huh," he said. Then he listened to my chest and thumped it. Finally, he tapped my knees until they jerked and then left the room. When Dr. Callahan returned, he carried a tray with a swabbing stick and a big needle just like the one in the picture.

"I'm pretty sure we're dealing with strep," he told my parents as I choked on the swab, "but I'll take a culture just to make sure. Call me tomorrow for the results. In the meantime, we had better start a series of penicillin shots— one today, another in a week, and a booster the week after." With that, the doctor rolled me on my side, exposed my rear, grabbed a disinfected fleshy part, and skewered it. I had been cautioned not to jump, but I couldn't help it. The fluid stung. The torture was over when I was alcoholed and Band-Aided.

As we left, Dad paid the admissions nurse some money and asked if he could send more next month. She agreed. Then we gathered Jeannie at the fish tank and drove home.

"Can I go out and play?" I asked Mom, two days after the injection.

"You must be joking. You'll have to stay indoors for another week."

"But I feel okay."

"If you're feeling better, how about finishing that stack of homework?"

Seven days later I returned to class. That was when Jeannie began to complain of a headache. Rebe saw her crying in the hallway and found me. Together, we helped her home. Mom said it was serious. Jeannie's face and hands had swollen.

"Do you have a sore throat?" Mom asked.

Jeannie nodded.

"When did it start?"

"When Shad was sick."

"Why didn't you tell me?"

"I thought it would go away."

Mom quickly wrapped Jeannie in a blanket and called Maudy Tyler to drive us to the doctor.

We were hustled to a special room where Dr. Callahan met us. He frowned as he examined Jeannie. "This little girl needs to be admitted into the hospital right now," he said. "She has a high fever and her blood pressure is at a dangerous level." Jeannie's kidneys were failing, he said. She had contracted a complication of strep called nephritis. Only quick action could get her kidneys functioning again.

Dr. Callahan was visibly shaken. So were my mother and Maudy. Dr. Callahan hadn't used the term "life-threatening," but his demeanor said it.

Maudy drove us straight to the hospital and offered to find my dad. Mom and I stayed with Jeannie as nurses and doctors rushed around her taking tests. Mom answered questions about Jeannie's medical history. This much was certain: when Jeannie had contracted strep, her kidneys had been attacked by the disease and were failing. Her body was filling with poisonous fluids that could kill her. That had caused her blood pressure to skyrocket, and the doctors were concerned that her heart would be damaged.

Three hours passed before Maudy brought Dad. The crush of medical people hurrying in and out had not changed. When Dad came in Mom cried as she hugged him. He insisted that she take a break and get some food. He called to me and asked that I go with her. Then he sat by Jeannie.

It was midnight when Mom and I returned. All had quieted and our family was alone. Jeannie had drifted asleep and, for the moment, was peaceful. Then Mom motioned us into the hall and directed us to the hospital chapel. "We need to pray for Jeannie," she said. She looked at Dad and he seemed to understand what she was asking.

"I don't know if I can, Eddie," he said. "I believe in God, but I've never offered a prayer like this." Mom reached out and took his hand, and we returned to Jeannie's room.

Jeannie had awakened and seemed relieved when she saw us. Mom stroked her and brushed the hair off her forehead. Then she looked at Dad. "It's okay," she whispered. "Your best will be enough."

Dad took a deep breath. He took Mom's hand in his right and mine in his left. Mom took my hand then, completing the circle around Jeannie's bed. We bowed our heads and closed our eyes. Dad squeezed our hands as if he was trying to draw strength from us. Then my father poured out his heart to God. I knew this was the prayer of his life. I felt him measure every word so that it was meaningful. I heard him yearn for language that could reach heaven and be worthy. He spoke to God as if God were there with us. I opened my eyes once to see if God had come into the room. Dad's petition was so honest I didn't doubt it was heard.

This is what he said: "Father in Heaven, you know how much we love this little girl." His voice broke. "If ever there was a time when our prayers needed to be heard and answered, it is tonight. You know our weaknesses. Help mine now. The words of my mouth can't express what I want to say. Please answer the prayer of my heart. The doctors are doing all they can for Jeannie, but it may not be enough. Nothing is beyond your power. Will you look tenderly on our little Jeannie? Please restore her to her family who love her so much. However you choose to heal her, help us to accept and acknowledge it. And if you choose to take her home, help us accept that, too."

We didn't move. None of us was dry-eyed. My father's plea was made. He had spoken to a god with ears and feelings and the capacity to help. Dad had addressed God as his "Father in Heaven," acknowledging his sonship. He wasn't a stranger, but a child petitioning a loving parent. I learned something that night, something I had never considered: My father knew and trusted God.

When Dad's simple prayer had ended, I felt a sweet presence enter that Idaho Falls hospital room. It comforted us. I had watched a man destitute of almost all worldly possessions, but rich in faith, call down the very powers of heaven on behalf of his daughter. And unseen things became real to me that night when I heard my father pray.

We gathered around Jeannie and wished her good night. Then Dad urged Mom and me to go home and sleep. He would stay the night. Mom said she'd rather sleep in the waiting room. That way we could take shifts. Dad relented. When I reached the door, I turned to my sister. "Bye, Jeannie. You'll be okay. I know it."

She smiled at me and said, "I know. The old man told me."

Mom and Dad took turns looking at each other with questioning expressions.

"What old man?" Mom asked. "Did you have a dream?"

"No, Mom," Jeannie insisted. "An old man came and held my hand. He said he would give me a present to make me better. Didn't you see him?"

"Sure we did, honey," Dad said. "Now you get some sleep." Dad waved us out of the room. "Come and trade with me at three."

Mom and I found the lumpy waiting room couches. At 2:45 A.M. she nudged me.

"Do you want to sleep or come with me to Jeannie's room?"

"I'll come."

When we opened the door, we saw my father patting Jeannie's hand. She was sleeping. Except for the dim lights of the monitors, the room was dark. A cold compress lay on Jeannie's forehead.

"Her temperature has dropped a little," Dad said. "She has slept, but she stirs a lot. Sometimes she calls out, afraid." Mom took his place and gestured for me to go with my father.

Dad and I stood for a moment outside the room. "You're a good boy to stay with us," Dad said.

I smiled at him. He put his arm around my shoulder and we started toward the waiting room. Suddenly, a loud cry came from Jeannie's room. We turned back and listened at the door. We heard my mother saying, "I'm here. I'm here."

Jeannie cried out, "I can't see you. I'm scared!"

"You don't have to be scared," Mom said. "I won't leave you."

"Where are you?"

"Here," Mom comforted her. "Can't you feel my hand and hear me?" Then Mom sang a soft lullaby. "Hush, little baby, don't say a word. Mama's gonna buy you a mockingbird. . . ."

Jeannie became quiet and Dad and I stepped back from the door. The seriousness of Jeannie's illness knifed through me. She might die, I thought. I felt my eyes become moist. Dad put his hand on my shoulder.

"Dad," I asked, "do you think God really heard our prayer?"

"I know God loves his children," Dad said. "He heard."

"But what if she dies?" My chin began to quiver.

Dad swallowed hard. "Then we'll allow him that, too. Jeannie is also his child."

"But I don't want her to die." I was crying hard.

"None of us do, son." Dad held me.

I whispered a searching question. "How do you know if your prayer is heard?"

"Listen," Dad said. I heard my mother's gentle song. "A still voice comes, if you will hear it. When you cry out in the dark, he finds a way to touch you, if you will feel."

I slept better on the lumpy sofa that night. In the morning, Jeannie was alert. Within a week her kidneys began to function again and she was discharged.

One day we heard Jeannie humming a beautiful, haunting melody. It had no words. We had never known Jeannie to be musical. In fact, we used to tease her about being tone deaf. But she hummed her song in clear tones and we couldn't help but wonder.

"Did you make it up?" Mom asked her.

"No, I learned it."

"From whom, honey?"

"From the old man in the hospital."

Home life revolved around Jeannie's recovery. The doctors worried about her heart. Dad moved her bed to the living room where she could be watched. For the next four weeks, she was ordered to lie on her back to keep the pressure off her heart. She was allowed to sit up only occasionally. During those weeks, Jeannie's teacher sent her homework. Often Jeannie's classmates came to visit. Neighbors arrived with meals, cards, and flowers. Two neighbors split a shift cleaning, cooking, and washing laundry. They never left us while Jeannie and our family healed.

Every day Jeannie improved a little. I remembered Dad saying that God could have healed Jeannie instantly, but he believed he hadn't so we could be blessed by our neighbors. He said God often chooses that way to heal because it blesses both the giver and the receiver. "That's a miracle," he said.

I witnessed another miracle the second day Jeannie was home. When I came home from school, I saw Sheila Shimmel tending her, feeding her Jell-O. I handed Jeannie the storybook her teacher had sent. Sheila began reading it to her. Then, every day for the next four weeks, Sheila came from school, sat on Jeannie's bed, and read her stories. Jeannie had company and Sheila learned to read.

The Auction

Dad tried to find humor in our financial situation. He said he had gone to "Heck" to get money. Jeannie's hospital bills amounted to over $4,000. The staggering sum exceeded his ability to pay. Only desperation could have persuaded him to work for a man like Heck Markham.

Dad begged long and hard for Mom's support, promising that he would make Heck the two hundred chairs and never work for the man again. He hoped to clear $3,000. Mom relented, but never felt at peace.

Dad and Mr. Markham shook hands on the deal. Mr. Markham predicted Dad would make thousands each month. Dad approached the arrangement with optimism. To purchase the lumber, Dad sold our car for $1,500. Five hundred dollars was used to fix up Grandpa's 1948 pickup that Dad had towed from Ucon. With new parts, the pickup ran in second and third gears.

Each night for the next two weeks, Dad ended eighteen-hour days after I had gone to sleep. When I awoke in the morning, he had already worked an hour or two. I watched him as he worked his power saw, cutting the boards to size. I learned to sand the rough areas and apply varnish. Dad put on the finishing touches. I was not allowed to operate the electric tools.

During those days of apprenticeship, I gained an appreciation for Dad's love of silly songs and cowboy tunes. His repertoire included "Ragtime Cowboy Joe," "Tumblin' Tumbleweeds," and "Ya Done Stomped on My Heart." He sang "Ghost Riders in the Sky" like the Sons of the Pioneers. I learned a simple harmony to "Mockingbird Hill" and sang with him.

One night we had a visitor.

"Zeb Mundy!" Dad exclaimed. "What brings you here?" Mr. Mundy had known Dad since we moved to Iona. Any time he could, Mr. Mundy sent Dad work and treated him well. Mr. Mundy was a big man, squarely built, with the thickest fingers I'd seen. His eyes creased at the corners, giving the appearance of a perpetual smile. People knew him for his big-heartedness.

Mr. Mundy slapped Dad on the back. "You haven't returned my phone calls since you started this Markham job."

"I'm sorry," Dad said. "Life's been hectic with Jeannie's illness, and this job's hanging over my head. But a few more days and I'll have it done." Dad tilted his head toward me. "You remember my son, Shadrach."

"I sure do!" Mr. Mundy said, reaching out and shaking my hand. "You know my boy, Delbert, don't you? Hey, Deb, come on over here." Debby was sitting in the car. Mr. Mundy turned back to Dad. "I've got a contract coming in December, Sam. I could use your help. I wouldn't want to take it unless I knew you were available."

"Can you give me a few days?" Dad said. "I'll be done then."

"You drive a hard bargain," Mr. Mundy laughed. Then he grew serious. "Have you collected anything from Markham yet?"

"No," Dad replied. "He said he'll pay me when I deliver the chairs."

"So you're extending him credit," Mr. Mundy said. Debby arrived then and Mr. Mundy brightened. "You boys know each other?"

"Yeah," said Debby. "Hi, Shad."

"Hi."

Both of us stood uncomfortably. Then I said, "Wanna see what we're making?"

"Okay." Debby followed me to the chairs. "You made all these?"

"My dad and I made them all." I showed him our shop, the tools, the finishing area. Debby asked questions; I answered. Soon, Mr. Mundy called him. Debby extended his hand and shook mine.

"Thanks," he said. "My dad thinks your dad is great."

After three weeks on the Markham job, I helped Dad haul the first one hundred and fifty chairs to Heck Markham's warehouse. Mr. Markham arrived as we unloaded the last of the chairs. He examined them with a jeweler's eye.

"Very nice," he said.

"Thanks, Heck," Dad replied. "I've brought an invoice for this first shipment—twenty dollars each, like we agreed, that's three thousand dollars. I can deliver the last fifty before the weekend."

Mr. Markham shuffled and said, "Sam, we have a problem." My heart sank. "You see," he began, "the buyer fell through. I can get another, but I can give you only five hundred dollars."

I saw my Dad's face go pale. "That's not what we agreed, Heck. I have no arrangement with any buyer except you. In fact, I have never known who you were selling the chairs to. My deal was with you alone. You gave me your word."

"Just a minute, Sam," Mr. Markham's voice rose. "I'm in a bind here and I'm not going to have you accusing me. We have nothing in writing. It's my word against yours. I'm willing to pay you what I can, but not a red cent more."

"That's not fair, Heck," Dad shot back. "If there was a problem, why didn't you tell me before I had committed? This will devastate my family. You know what we've been through."

"I'd like to be sympathetic," Mr. Markham said, "but I can't be responsible for everybody's family. This is business and all I can offer is five hundred dollars. If you think you have a market for a hundred and fifty chairs at twenty dollars apiece, be my guest!"

I watched my father's eyes brim with tears as he held out his hand and took Heck Markham's five hundred dollars. Dad looked at the crumpled green paper in his hand and said, "You've got more money than anyone in town, Heck. There's no doubt you'll get richer because of this. But this is below even you. How can you break your word straight-faced and find a way to feel good about it? How can you live with yourself knowing you kicked a man when he was down?"

Mr. Markham brought his face to Dad's with a look as evil as I'd ever seen. "Get out of my building. How dare you lecture me on morality? If you didn't want the money, why did you take it? Show me one law I've broken. My conscience is clear. Business is business. I'm not running a charity ward. Get out!"

Dad and I exited and said nothing all the way home. The $3,000 loss had a terrible impact. Jeannie's medical bills remained unpaid; Dad had spent a month working on Mr. Markham's contract. All he had to show for his effort was five hundred dollars, a broken-down pickup, and fifty unsold chairs.

I lay in bed that night listening to my mother and father cry. Darkness brooded over our home. Jeannie stopped singing. Mom had to borrow money from Maudy Tyler for groceries. She cried the rest of the day. Word went out and soon food and clothing appeared on our doorstep.

During those hard November days, Mom and Dad often bundled in warm coats and walked the dark Iona streets. They held hands and talked. Slowly, that balm spread over Jeannie and me and we began to recover.

One day Dad burst into the house and yelled, "Eddie! Come here!"

Mom came running.

"Look at this!" Dad handed her a note from Zeb Mundy.

Mom read it out loud. "Sam, I need your help building joists for a couple of houses in Pocatello. Don't turn me down on this one. If we do a good job we'll get the contract for the whole development. Can you start right away? It will take a week and I'll pay you in advance. I heard about Markham. It's just a suggestion, but you might want to sell the last of the chairs at the Idaho Falls auction. Christmas should be a good time to move them."

Mom danced around the room. I turned a somersault. Jeannie bounced on her bed until Mom told her to stop. That week Dad busied himself building the joists and finishing the fifty chairs.

Saturdays were auction days in Idaho Falls. Two trips sold thirty of Dad's chairs at twenty-two dollars a piece. Each Saturday we filled the pickup with chairs and drove to Idaho Falls. The pickup seemed to protest each time Dad shoved it into gear, but somehow he found a way to keep it running.

During those weeks Jeannie convalesced to the point that she could sit up in bed and walk a few steps each day. Encouraged, Mom suggested a family outing—something we had not experienced in a long time—to the auction. Dr. Callahan agreed, but cautioned that Jeannie be wrapped warmly and not walk.

I helped Dad load the last twenty chairs into the pickup and rope them to the bed. When we finished, he returned to the house and carried Jeannie to the truck. Mom's lap was where Jeannie sat as we all crowded into the cab. The truck's heater had died, so we wore double socks and flannels. We sang carols the whole way.

The auction was held in a tented area with rows of folding chairs on a sawdust floor. Mom and Jeannie sat blanketed in the front row. Dad and I unloaded the chairs and spoke to the auctioneer. He was a tall man, gaunt like a scarecrow, with an engaging laugh. When he spoke into his microphone he could make his voice halt and hurry and otherwise present his wares like no one's I had heard. I discovered that buyers have a sign language—small gestures, a nod, a wave—that conveyed their commitment.

Because Christmas had summoned a gaggle of bidders, business was brisk. Laws of supply and demand ruled. Used toasters, which should have gone for a dollar, went for two; archery sets were a steal at ten; and Dad's chairs sold for twenty-five dollars each!

Then the auctioneer opened the case of an old violin. When he lifted it out, its strings sagged like the reins on a resting buggy. He blew the dust away, revealing scars. The edges were battered. He cracked a scoffing smile and checked his watch.

"What am I bid?" he almost laughed. "One dollar? Two? Who'll make it three?"

A hand went up from the back of the crowd. The auctioneer hooded his eyes and pounded his gavel. "Sold to that elderly gentleman." All heads turned as the old man came forward. A few whispered, a few laughed low.

"It's him!" Jeannie gasped.

"Who, honey?" Mom asked. "Who is it?"

"The old man—the one who came to see me in the hospital."

Dad looked up. "Ephraim? Ephraim Shimmel?"

Mr. Shimmel smiled at Dad and tipped his hat to my mother. "Mornin'," he said. "Nice day for an auction." Mr. Shimmel shuffled toward the auctioneer's table on his cane.

Mom nudged Dad. "Go help him, Sam!"

Dad went to Mr. Shimmel's side and took his elbow.

"I'm okay, now," Mr. Shimmel said when they arrived. "Go on back to your family." The old man patted Dad on the back.

Jeannie was big-eyed. Mom whispered for me to close my mouth. We thought he existed only in a sick child's dream. Mr. Shimmel dug through his wallet and retrieved three one-dollar bills. Then he took the instrument in his hands, lovingly dusted it with his handkerchief, and tuned the strings. He raised the old violin to his chin and played a melody haunting and beautiful. At once, Jeannie began to hum along. We recognized the tune immediately. The gentle strain pierced me. I looked around. Others were sitting forward. Some looked puzzled. When Mr. Shimmel lowered his bow, the audience remained silent. Then someone stood and began to clap. He was followed by another, then another. I looked around in amazement. Grown people were crying.

One man shouted, "I'll give $1,000, if you'll sell me that violin."

Another yelled, "I'll give two thousand!"

"I'll give three!" came another voice.

The auctioneer stood speechless, and the crowd cheered.

Mr. Shimmel waved off the offers and set the violin back in its case. Then he turned to Jeannie. The crowd hushed. Slowly, the old man hobbled to my sister and placed the case on her lap. None of us spoke. Jeannie looked up at Mom seeming to ask for permission. Mom tearfully nodded. Jeannie rubbed her hands over the case, looked up into Mr. Shimmel's eyes, and smiled.

"Thanks, Ephraim," said Dad.

Mr. Shimmel looked embarrassed. "No," he said. "Thank you, Sam Widener."

I wondered what had happened, but couldn't form a question. Within a few days I had an answer.

A Test of Integrity

I TURNED TWELVE. I knew there would be no presents. Mom had done all she could just to provide a cake.

Billy's dad owned a Christmas tree lot. One day Billy arrived with an enormous pine strapped to his Radio Flyer. The big, toothy smile he couldn't conceal almost broke his face. Dad sawed off the trunk square, trimmed off the bottom branches, and fashioned a wooden base to support it. We set it by Jeannie's bed in the front room and covered it with paper decorations, strings of popcorn, and gingerbread men. Billy's tree brought a feeling of Christmas into our home. Soon Christmas music rose from Mom's record player. Jeannie learned to tune her violin to the records and play along. We especially loved "Hark! The Herald Angels Sing" because the tune was Mendelssohn's.

For Christmas presents, Jeannie drew pictures of our family in winter scenes. She wrapped them in taped newspaper and placed them under the tree.

Turning twelve proved pivotal. A seed of unselfishness had sprouted within me from the examples of my family. I had no money or talent, so I gave presents of what I could. Leon Bitner's mother held an indoor garage sale each December. Leon had never forgiven me for taking Rebe from him, but he considered us even when I traded him my bag of cat's-eyes for a book of Christmas songs for the violin. I warmed inside when I saw Jeannie's excitement and heard her play the melodies.

I couldn't think of anything to give Dad, so I spent an afternoon cutting a felled cherry tree into winter fuel.

"You're a real man now," Dad said, admiring the pile of logs. "You've learned how to give." Then his eyes twinkled. "Do you really want to feel some happiness?"

"Sure, Dad."

"I know a family who needs this wood more than we. Let's load it onto the truck and take it to them." He looked so excited I couldn't turn him down.

When we had loaded the wood, Dad drove down Main Street and stopped in front of the streetlight where the bats flew. "Go ask Mr. Shimmel where he wants us to stack this wood," he said. I felt awkward. I realized I had seen Mr. Shimmel up close just once and Billy's description of the man still haunted me, although I suspected it wasn't true.

I knocked on the Shimmels' door.

Nothing.

I looked around at Dad, who gestured to try again. I knocked louder.

A voice inside answered, "What's all the ruckus? Just come in! It's open!"

Dad waved me in as he arranged the load. Gingerly, I pushed open the creaky door. The Shimmel home was dimly lit. When my eyes adjusted, I saw a gray-haired man sitting in a wheelchair at the far end of the room. Mr. Shimmel eyed me.

"We met at the auction," I said, spying a lonely cane near the door. He wheeled forward until he could see my father in the yard. "We've brought you some wood," I said. "Would you like us to pile it at the side of your house?"

I became uneasy when he didn't answer. Mr. Shimmel looked at the truck, then at me. "It's okay, Ephraim," Dad shouted. "It's Sam Widener. This is my son, Shadrach. He's cut this wood for you. Where do you want it?"

Mr. Shimmel's eyes became moist. I discovered I didn't know my father as well as I'd thought. He had made this charitable trip before, and the two neighbors knew each other well.

"The side of the house will be fine, Sam," Mr. Shimmel said. He dabbed his eyes with a handkerchief and looked at me. "You chopped all this?"

"Yes, sir."

"You're a kind boy, Shadrach Widener, just like your father." He reached out and squeezed my hand. "I'm proud to know you. Come inside when you're finished."

Dad and I stacked the wood and entered the humble Shimmel home. Sheila came from the kitchen and asked us to sit on the davenport. We sank deep into the springless sofa and waited. I surveyed the shadowy dwelling. Doors led to the kitchen, a bedroom, and a bathroom. These, along with the living room where we sat, made up the entire Shimmel home. Except for the davenport, the only furniture was two folding chairs, a lamp, and an orange crate for the lamp. The sole source of heating appeared to be a rock fireplace. Several pans caught water from a leaky ceiling.

Mr. Shimmel returned with hot cocoa. He balanced a tray on his knees as he wheeled toward us. He asked Dad how Jeannie fared and made him promise to thank my mother for the dress she had mended for Sheila. Dad promised.

"I can't remember your needing a wheelchair, Ephraim," Dad commented.

"Been pretty sick lately," said Mr. Shimmel. "The poor old legs don't work much any more."

"You seeing a doctor?" asked Dad.

"He gave me this buggy," Mr. Shimmel patted his wheelchair. "I spent some time in the hospital a while back. Seen your daughter one night. Taught her a little song to make her feel better."

"We didn't know it was you, Ephraim. Thank you," Dad said.

"I was having a bad night," said Mr. Shimmel. "I couldn't sleep. Nurses don't like it when I wander the halls." He paused. "Your little girl looked pretty sick. Figured I ought to do something."

"That's why you came to the auction?" Dad asked. Mr. Shimmel nodded. "How did you get there with those legs?"

"Wasn't easy."

Dad looked as astonished as I felt. He stopped pressing for answers. Mr. Shimmel beckoned Sheila to retrieve something from the bedroom.

"Give Jeannie this." Mr. Shimmel handed Dad a knitted scarf, neatly folded and tied with a ribbon.

"The violin was more than enough, Ephraim."

"Please, Sam," Mr. Shimmel insisted.

Dad accepted the gift and we donned our coats. Dad said, "Shad and I will patch those leaks in your roof before we leave." When we left the Shimmel home I had learned more about Christmas and neighboring than I'd ever known.

Two days later, Billy came bearing gifts.

"Here, Shad," he said, grinning. He couldn't wait for Christmas morning, so he made me open his present early.

"A baseball glove!" I exclaimed.

"It's my old one," Billy said. "I'm getting a new one."

"How do you know?"

"I peeked," he said. "Can I see Jeannie?"

I took Billy to the living room.

"Hi, Billy."

"Hi, Jeannie," Billy replied. "Uh, Shad, can I have a moment alone?"

"Sure." I exited, but listened at the door.

"What are you doing?" Mom asked.

"Shhh! I'm trying to hear." Mom dropped her baking and stepped to the door to listen with me. She was a sucker for juicy news.

"Jeannie," Billy began clumsily, "I brought you this present. I hope it makes you feel better."

"What is it?" Jeannie asked excitedly.

"Open it and see."

Jeannie tore at the wrapping and pulled out a stuffed bear in plaid trousers. "He's like my other bear!" Jeannie exclaimed, hugging it.

"His name is *Mister* Muggins."

Mom couldn't contain herself. She burst into the room. "William Van Olpin, you're the nicest boy I know!" Then she kissed him on the forehead.

Billy's face was as red as holly berries. "I've got to be going. 'Bye, Shad. 'Bye, Jeannie."

"Wait!" I yelled. "I've got something for you." I rushed to my room and returned with my remaining marbles— the agates and steelies. "Merry Christmas, Billy," I said, shoving the bag in his hand.

Billy received the treasure. "Oh, Shad! These are too nice. I can't take these."

"Yes, you can," I insisted. "They're yours."

As he left smiling, Jeannie called after him, "'Bye, Billy. Thank you!"

After that, Mister and Missus Muggins were never apart, except when Jeannie slept. Then they lay on either side of Jeannie's pillow.

I told Mom I wanted to give Rebe something special. One day she handed me her Mendelssohn record. "Give her this," she said. "I have a feeling Rebe has an appreciation for beautiful music." I tried to protest, but she insisted. After I wrapped it and delivered it to Rebe, she gave me a pie she had made. Many Christmases have found us eating pie to Mendelssohn and candlelight.

I had nothing to give Mom, so each night I sat at her feet and pushed the pedals of her sewing machine with my hands. That gift was returned.

My coat was worn and I had outgrown it. Without my knowing, Mom had salvaged scraps of cloth and pieced them together into a warm, colorful coat. When I received it as a belated birthday present I couldn't believe how beautiful it was—or that she had fashioned it without my knowing. It fit perfectly. Large buttons down the front fastened it snugly to my body. The ample collar could be raised to shelter my neck. I threw my arms around my mother and thanked her over and over. She pretended it was no big deal, anyone could have made it, she said. She tried to hide a smile and rushed me outside.

Warm inside my multicolored wrap, I hardly noticed the cold. Then Jeepers Craddock walked by. I tried to ignore him, but he strolled into the yard.

"Hi, Shad."

"Hi, Jeepers. Where's the gang?"

"I dunno," he said. He was shivering. His coat was tattered like my old one, except it had no buttons and its thinness made it appear like holes held together with thread. His mother was single and poor. Maybe that longing for family was why he had tied himself to Debby.

"Nice coat," he said.

"My mom made it for me."

He hunched his shoulders and said 'bye. When he did, I was sorry I'd hated him.

That evening I slipped into the house and hung my old wrap in the closet. Mom saw me.

"Where's your new coat?"

I hesitated a moment, fearing she would become angry. "I gave it away." I said, shuffling my feet. I looked at the floor.

Mom's voice became soft. "Why would you do that?"

"Jeepers . . . Jerry Craddock has no coat. I had two. He looked like he was freezing."

Mom sat and held my hands. "Why didn't you give him your old coat?" But she seemed to know the answer. She brought me close and held me in her arms. "Of course you couldn't. Of course you couldn't."

Jeannie had taught herself to play the Christmas carols from the book I'd given her. None of us had to wonder if Jeannie had talent; her gift was evident early on. In a matter of days, she and the violin had become one. I didn't know what the word "prodigy" meant when Mom and Dad started using it. Without instruction, Jeannie demonstrated a genius for fingering positions and bowing techniques. Within a week, we were hard-pressed to imagine her without a violin in her hand. It was like she was born with it. Even the awkward chin rest, the bane of the beginner, fit her as part of her body.

More astonishing, the music was healing her. Almost from the moment she placed her bow on the strings she became more animated. Her coloring improved. She began to gain weight and strength. At her next visit, Dr. Callahan was so impressed that he told my parents to find a way to keep Jeannie playing. "It's doing more to cure her than any medicine I could give her," he said.

Jeannie had been blessed with a rare musical gift. We all knew it. Coupled with the fact that Jeannie's recovery had become dependent on her music, my parents felt an urgency to provide her with an opportunity. In the few days since the auction, Jeannie had managed to devour all the violin materials we could place before her, even the method books Dad had ferreted from secondhand stores. Nothing my parents did could keep pace with Jeannie's ability. What she needed were lessons and a teacher.

Late one night, as I lay awake in bed, I heard my parents discussing Jeannie.

"It's beyond us," I heard Dad say. "I don't know how to afford a teacher. We have no extra money and the hospital bills are seriously delinquent."

"Why not ask Ephraim Shimmel to teach her?" Mom suggested.

"He's too frail. You should have seen him. No, we'll have to think of another way."

"Maybe I could take in more ironing and sewing," Mom said.

"You're already putting in long days," Dad said. "Where would you find the time?"

Silence followed. Then I heard my mother whisper, "Maybe Heck Markham—maybe his heart has softened."

Dad raised his voice, "That man is as unfeeling as anyone I have ever known. No way would he change his mind, not even for a sick little girl. I never want to see or speak to him again."

The mere mention of Heck Markham's name still sapped Dad's energy for hours at a time. What our family had suffered at Heck Markham's hands was enough to embitter the most saintly. The suggestion was dropped.

❧ ❧ ❧

"Can't I please go to the Christmas pageant tonight?" Jeannie cried. Each year our church reenacted the Christmas story with local talent. This was our first Christmas in Iona. We had anticipated the pageant the entire month.

"What do you think?" Mom asked Dad. "Maybe we should stay home."

"Pleeease?" Jeannie begged.

Dad sat beside her. "You're just getting well . . . ." He looked into her eyes and melted. "Okay," he sighed, "I guess we can bundle you up."

Jeannie clapped. So did I. We knew the pageant would end with a visitor from the North Pole bringing bags of candy, oranges, and peanuts. For the rest of the day we belted out carols while Mom sewed shepherd costumes. Jeannie tried on hers first.

"Sam!" Mom shouted. "Come look how adorable!"

Dad came in from his work and gushed praises. He said she looked exactly like a shepherd. Suddenly, Jeannie started swaying and her eyes rolled back.

"Eddie!" Dad yelled. "Catch her. She's fainting!"

Mom grabbed Jeannie just as her knees buckled.

"Lay her down and take off her turban," Dad said. Mom had improvised a shepherd's headdress with a scarf and an elastic. When the elastic was removed and the blood rushed back to Jeannie's head, she recovered, except for the scarlet crease along her hairline.

"Maybe we'll just let your pretty hair be your hat," Mom suggested. Jeannie didn't argue. Neither did I, since I knew I was the next to be dressed in a shepherd's costume.

I can still recall the night of December 21, 1961. We shepherds squeezed into the pickup with our parents and drove toward the church building where the pageant would be held. Fresh snow lay like a wool blanket, reflecting the merry reds and greens of lights that decorated houses. The snow crunched beneath the tires, leaving the lone blemish on the white road. Dad had thrown sandbags into the truck's bed for traction. Because it had no defroster, Dad had to continually wipe fog from our breath off the inside windshield. Soon we turned onto the street that led to the church.

"Sam, look!" Mom said, motioning Dad to stop.

"What?"

"The light is on in Heck Markham's warehouse. He's in there." Mom pointed to a lit bulb marking the warehouse door.

"I know what you're thinking," Dad said, "but I can't do it. I won't grovel—especially not to a man like that."

"It's not groveling," Mom said. "It's asking for what is owed you." A dense silence settled on us in the cold truck. I could see my father weighing Mom's words. Mom urged him again. "You won't know unless you try. All he can do is turn us down. Besides, it's Christmas. Maybe he will have softened."

My father looked at her doubtfully and pulled the pickup back into the street. "Okay," he said, "one more try."

Dad mouthed what he would say as we drove the long road to the warehouse.

"I'd better go in first," he said.

"We'll all go in together," Mom insisted. Dad didn't argue. He set his jaw and stared through the windshield.

When we pulled up to the warehouse, a terrible sight made me chill. In the shadows at the side of the warehouse, a solitary figure hung from the smashed door of a car. "It's Mr. Markham!" I gasped. Judging from the tracks in the snow, Mr. Markham's car had spun out of control and collided into his building. The crumpled hood had jarred open, spewing steam into the air.

"Don't look, Jeannie." Mom said, covering my sister's eyes. Then, whispering to Dad, she asked, "Is he dead?"

A low moan from the demolished automobile answered her question. I saw my father sit forward. Mom said nothing. Jeannie had pushed away Mom's hand. No one jumped to help; no one panicked; no one offered a word of regret. We all remained quiet in the pickup.

"Sam?" Mom said, putting her hand on Dad's.

His knuckles were white on the steering wheel.

Dad looked at her.

"What are we going to do?" Mom said.

He gazed out the window. "So many times I've wished for something like this to happen. I've cursed this man and swore if he ever needed help I would turn and walk away. And here he is."

I stared at Mr. Markham, bloody, hanging out of his grand car. I recalled his cheating my dad. I remembered my father's face when he took the five hundred dollars. I thought of the evening my mom and dad wept as they tried to hold together lives devastated by the decision of that man. I agreed with my father: If anyone had cause to turn away, it was Dad.

Mom said, "If you let how you feel dictate what you do, Heck Markham's won. Who he is doesn't matter; who you are does."

Dad gazed at her. All the hurt showed in his face. "I thought I knew myself," he said. "Maybe I'm not who I thought."

"Sam Widener," Mom said softly, "I know who you are." She touched his cheek. "We'll help that man like we would any other. And, after all that, if we walk away with nothing else, we'll have our integrity . . . and that's enough to start over."

All of us, except Jeannie, who was instructed to remain in the truck, gathered around Mr. Markham's car. Dad pried open the door and I helped him pull Mr. Markham loose. Then Dad took his shoulders while Mom and I lifted his legs.

"Eddie," Dad said, "this is not good for your leg. You'll be limping for a week. Let Shad do it."

"He's too heavy," Mom replied. "I'll be okay." Mom grimaced as she and I hefted Mr. Markham's heavy legs and inched toward the truck. A deep gash ran across his forehead. Blood ran onto Dad's hands and coat. The leg I carried had a jagged rip. I tried not to look at it. With some effort, we hoisted Mr. Markham onto the truck bed. I volunteered to hold him as Dad drove us to the hospital. We wrapped him in Jeannie's blanket. She and Mom huddled together inside Mom's coat. I lay Mr. Markham's bleeding head on my lap and pushed on his wound with Dad's handkerchief. The gash vented steam into my face.

Dad shoved the truck into gear, and we jerked toward the hospital in Idaho Falls. The cold froze my ears and nose. Once I thought Mr. Markham had died, but I prayed, "Please don't let him die here on my lap!" Then he uttered a mournful sound. Death had not yet come to Heck Markham. The jarring of the truck cracked open an eyelid, exposing the waxy part of his eyeball. I shuddered.

I looked at the ashen eye and imagined he might open his eyes and attack me. I held my breath and forced my finger to his eye and shut it. At that moment he coughed up blood and I screamed. Dad hit the brakes, but I motioned him on. For the rest of the trip to the hospital, I turned my head away and bit my tongue.

A flurry of medics hustled Mr. Markham into the emergency room. We tried to warm ourselves in the waiting area. My parents gave details of the accident to a nurse and two policemen. Mr. Markham had no family, no one to contact. We Wideners were all the family he would have that night. We would wait until the early hours of December 22 before we received word of his condition.

I was still dressed like a shepherd when I awoke on a waiting room couch at 2:45 A.M. I heard a doctor speaking with my parents.

"Thanks for staying," he was saying. "Mr. Markham is out of danger and conscious now. He has suffered a concussion and lost considerable blood. Any delay would have cost him his life. We'll keep him hospitalized for a week, but we expect a full recovery."

My parents thanked the doctor and prepared to go home. At that moment, two orderlies wheeled Mr. Markham through the room toward an elevator.

"There he is now," the doctor said. "Do you want to talk to him?"

"No. Maybe later," Dad said.

"Just a minute," a weak voice stopped the orderlies. "I want to see that man." From his gurney Mr. Markham pointed a bony finger at my father.

Dad walked toward him.

Mr. Markham eyed my father. "You think this changes things, don't you?"

My father stood silent.

"It changes nothing. Do you hear me? It changes nothing."

The elevator bell rang. The orderlies pushed the gurney toward the elevator, and Dad reached out to stop them. Then he regarded the broken man lying before him and smiled.

"You're wrong, Heck," he replied. Then he straightened. "It changes everything."

At 3:00 A.M., we went home warm.

The Price of Lessons

ON OCCASION I HAVE FELT THE NEED to petition heaven with real intent, hoping that my words would be heard and answered. I have yearned for the ability to address God as my father had, with the tongue of an angel. I have twice witnessed pleadings that penetrated the gates of heaven and drew down its power. The first was when I heard my father pray for the life of his daughter; the second was when he prayed for her lessons.

In the early morning hours of December 22, 1961, I awoke to the soft sounds of my parents' voices discussing Jeannie's health and talent.

"Sam," I heard my mother whisper, "Is there any way we can afford to give Jeannie lessons?"

"I've racked my brain," Dad said. "the music is healing her. When she plays the violin her face lights up and she seems stronger."

"Not to mention her genius for music," Mom said.

"We've nothing left to sell," Dad said. "The car, our better furniture, your china are gone. I suppose we could sell the pickup."

"That's not practical," Mom said. "How would you work? Or what if there was another emergency? What about my sewing machine? It's worth something."

"We need the income you get from your sewing," Dad said. "Selling the sewing machine doesn't make any more sense than selling the pickup."

My parents discussed possible solutions for a while longer. They had no resource, no money, nothing left to sell.

"It's a load too heavy for us," Mom said. "All we can do is give it to God."

I came to the doorway of the bedroom and peered around the corner. My parents kneeled at chairs. They held hands. I expected a miracle. I'd seen one before. Then my father prayed. I remember his words carried a feeling that charged through me.

"We pray for the health of Jeannie," he said. "Music will heal her. Just to have a little money for lessons, that's all we ask. We have nothing left to sell." Then he paused, and with a voice of meekness he said, "I offer anything for lessons for my little girl."

I looked at the clock. It read 6:07 A.M. That meant my parents had spent the better part of the night seeking an answer. The accident, the hospital, all that happened last night now seemed like a dream. When the clock read 8:14, the phone in the kitchen was ringing.

I stumbled toward it and told the caller I would rouse my father from bed.

Zeb Mundy was the caller. He joked with Dad about his banker's hours and how rich people can afford to sleep in. Dad seemed amused but weary. Suddenly, I saw Dad reach for a chair.

"Yes! Yes, of course. I can start right away. I'll be right down to talk with you." Dad hung up the phone and called for Mom.

She staggered from the bedroom in her bathrobe, her hair in a tangle. Dad swooped her up in his arms and twirled her around the kitchen.

Mom was awake now. "Sam! Are you crazy? Put me down."

Dad gave her a dip and sat her on a chair. "We're going to be okay! Zeb Mundy just called. He offered me a six-month contract making joists." He hefted me, then Jeannie, who had emerged from the bedroom rubbing her eyes. "I'll bet we'll see some presents under that bare Christmas tree!"

We didn't even have time to react. Dad darted for the bedroom. "Can't talk now! I've got to get down there. Shad, I'll be back by noon with the lumber. Can you help me this afternoon?"

"Sure, Dad," I said. But I don't think he heard, because he was dressed and out the door before any of us had a chance to breathe.

"Mom?" Jeannie said. "Does this mean I can ask for a music book?"

Mom hesitated. "Yes, honey," she replied carefully. "I guess that's what it means."

I hadn't allowed myself to think of presents. I hadn't expected there would be any. I didn't even want to ask. So when Mom danced through the kitchen and asked me what I wanted, I had no answer. By noon I knew.

Last Christmas my parents had given me a dollar pocketwatch. During the summer, however, I had broken it. Since then, I carried it in my pocket just for looks. "I'd like my watch fixed for Christmas," I said. Mom smiled, hugged me, and told me to leave it by the phone so she could remember to take it to town.

Dad brought the lumber and I helped him stack it under a lean-to he had fashioned. Then work began on the joists. All day and into the nights of December 22 and 23, I helped my father build joists, knowing that if he met his first quota by the following afternoon, he and Mom could break away before the stores closed on Christmas Eve.

By midnight of December 23, I fell exhausted into my bed. The sound of my father's table saw and the pounding of his hammer echoed through the night. When Mom shook me at 7:00 A.M., I rose to the same sounds. Dad had worked all night. I guessed that he had slept two hours in the last two days. Mom fed me breakfast and I took some to Dad, who insisted on eating as he worked.

"Dad," I said. "Can't you rest a minute? You're not looking well."

"I'll be okay, Shad. I've got to deliver these joists this afternoon so I can get paid."

I steadied the long two-by-fours as Dad cut them to length. Then I picked up the scraps and piled them in a bin. I felt useless when the time came for hammering nails. Dad was much faster and stronger. He could pound four nails to my one. From the kitchen I heard Mom singing as Jeannie played Christmas melodies on her violin. The fresh aroma of gingerbread floated into the shop and mingled with the scent of cut lumber. Dad and I had stopped talking. He seemed to be using all his energy to stay awake.

I have often relived the moments that followed. Perhaps I wasn't paying attention, maybe I looked away, possibly I didn't hold the board tight—I will never know what made the board buck in my hands. I remember it bolted out of my grasp and struck me in the chest. When I picked myself up I was unhurt but surprised. I saw my father falter toward the doorway. His ashen face told me something terrible had happened. Then I saw blood spurting from his right hand. Before I could react, Mom was yelling, "Shad, stay with Jeannie. I'll call you from the hospital."

A long Christmas Eve afternoon had Jeannie and me waiting and wondering about our father's welfare. I encouraged Jeannie to play her violin, but she wouldn't. I busied away the afternoon sweeping up the sawdust and tidying the shop. I took a soapy bucket and washed the blood from the floor. Mostly, Jeannie and I worried, wishing our parents would return or call. When evening came, I made Jeannie a supper of tomato soup and bread, then I washed the dishes and straightened up the kitchen. My broken watch still lay by the phone.

December's darkness blanketed Iona when Mom returned home. She bundled us in coats and blankets for another cold ride to the hospital.

"The saw cut through the nerves in your dad's hand," she said as she drove.

"Can they sew him back together?" Jeannie asked.

"Yes, honey," Mom's voice quieted, "but he has lost most of the use of his right hand."

"Dad's right-handed," I said.

"Yes, Shad. The doctors had to perform emergency surgery. They saved his hand from being severed completely, but he will have to learn to use his left."

When we arrived at the hospital Mom gathered Jeannie in her arms and we walked to Dad's room.

"Be very quiet," Mom instructed us. "He might be sleeping."

Dad's room was at the end of a long hallway. When we walked in I could see his hand bandaged in bulky white gauze. He slept restlessly. Mom sat Jeannie on a chair and I sat beside her. Mom went to Dad and kissed him on the forehead. He opened his eyes.

"I'm sorry," she said. "I didn't mean to wake you."

"It's all right. I can't sleep very well anyway." Then Dad looked away. "Some answer."

"What do you mean?"

"We prayed for a miracle and got this."

"That's the painkiller talking, Sam," she said. "Let it go for now."

But Dad continued. "All I wanted was to support my family and give my little girl lessons. Is it too much to ask for lessons? For her health? What did I do wrong?"

"Everything will work out. It always has."

"How can you say that?" Dad said. "Look at me. How can I work with only one hand?"

I couldn't take it. I had never seen my father so hurt. I walked out into the hallway and wiped away the tears from my eyes. I was sure this was somehow my fault. I rehearsed the event over and over in my mind. I wished we could go back in time.

A strong hand startled me. "Shad Widener, isn't it?"

I turned. "Mr. Mundy? Debby?"

"Hi, Shad," Debby said. "We heard about the accident. Is this the right room?"

I nodded.

Mr. Mundy cracked the door and stepped inside. "Kinda laid up, aren't you, Sam?"

"Zeb!" Dad said, surprised. "How'd you know I was here?"

"Oh, I got my ways," Mr. Mundy laughed. "I called around. This is a pretty lousy way to impress your boss."

"Yeah," Dad said. "Some luck. I guess you can see I won't be able to finish that contract for you."

"Appears so," Mr. Mundy said. Then he turned to my mother. "He's feeling sorry for himself, isn't he?"

Mom looked at Dad.

"Never mind," Mr. Mundy stopped her. "I can see he is. You can tell him for me that I can't have a plant manager with a bad attitude."

"Plant . . . what?" Dad said.

"That's right. I'm offering you the full-time position of plant manager. Of course, you'll have to learn to write with your left hand!" Then Mr. Mundy became serious. "Sam, you've earned this. I've never had a better worker or one more honest."

Dad didn't have time to respond.

Mr. Mundy grinned at Mom. "He's not going to make this easy for me is he?"

Mom just stared at him.

"All right!" Mr. Mundy sounded firm. He looked at Dad. "I'll pay your price. You've got me against a wall. I've got to have you and you know it. That's a lousy bargaining position for me. Here's what I'll do. You put a down payment on that house you're renting and fill it with some nice furniture. You can afford it now. A car comes with this job and I'm going to give you ten percent of the profits. But not a penny more!"

Mom took Dad's good hand and squeezed it. They both had tears in their eyes. I could see they wanted to say thank you but couldn't. Mr. Mundy stepped close to Dad's bed and choked back some emotions of his own. "My son's got something for you."

Then Debby handed Dad an envelope. "This is for you, Mr. Widener," Debby said.

Dad gave the envelope to Mom. She immediately covered her eyes and wept. "Eddie? What is it?"

"It's an advance, Sam," Mr. Mundy replied. "You can pay it back out of your share of the profits. It should be enough to pay your hospital bills and then some. Spend it how you want."

I saw my mother and father look at each other, then at Jeannie. I knew exactly how they would use the money.

Ovation

REBE TOUCHED MY HAND, anticipating the conclusion of Jean Van Olpin's performance. I glanced at the beautiful woman who had given herself to me twenty-five years ago. In every way she had lived her vow to love and honor me, in sickness and in health, for richer and poorer. I remembered our standing at a small grave where we laid our precious Cynthia, who lived just five days, and experiencing the worst life has to offer. But I also recalled our wonderful children who followed, gathered around a Thanksgiving table, singing, laughing, and my thinking that life could offer nothing better. Our children had left Iona. Sam and Annie had started families of their own, and Lillie attended school out-of-state. I wished they could have come to see their Aunt Jean perform, but I held telegrams of congratulations from each. Rebe and I never moved from our little town in southeastern Idaho. Instead, we bought the white house from my parents, who lived with us until they died. There we had reared our family on the salary I earned from Zeb's Truss Joist, where I had been employed since my youth.

I watched Jean Van Olpin's bow leap over the strings as she attacked the lilting third movement of Mendelssohn's violin concerto. The quick melody seemed to awaken listeners from the subdued second movement. They sat up straight or leaned forward. Truly, Jean was the Nightingale. Mendelssohn's bold cadenza brought the audience, in one motion, from their seats, applauding the soloist's performance. We all knew we had experienced something remarkable.

At the last note, Jean Van Olpin held her bow to the strings, as was her style, and slowly lowered it to her side. Her violin followed. She bowed and acknowledged the orchestra, who had also risen in appreciation.

I scanned the audience. Front and center sat Delbert Mundy and his wife, Libby, holding their new granddaughter, who had her grandmother's lovely brown eyes. When his father retired, Delbert had taken the reins of the company. Under Delbert's leadership the company had grown tenfold. From the profits he created an endowment for the arts in my father's name and made the concert possible.

I saw Jerry Craddock sitting with his wife and six children. He owned a clothing store in Idaho Falls and was known to give coats to needy children at Christmas time.

William Van Olpin, whom we called Uncle Billy, sat with his two children. They took an active role in Jean's career, especially Uncle Billy himself, who was her manager. He and Jeannie developed a charity for children's hospitals, to give toys to sick children. They called it "Mister and Missus Muggins Toys."

Sheila Shimmel moved from Iona to Colorado to live with an aunt. Her grandfather died in the spring of 1962. I missed him. I tried to imagine what his reaction to the night's event might have been.

I took Rebe's hand and stood up with the audience. I searched for the time and pulled a shiny watch from my vest. It was 9:30 P.M. In 1961 one could buy such a watch for a dollar. This particular one was priceless. Its inscription read, "Happy Christmas. Love, Mom and Dad."

"Encore, encore!" the audience shouted.

The soloist bowed her consent. The orchestra left the stage so that Jeannie stood alone. Spotlights from the right and from the left haloed her. She lifted her bow and the room hushed. Then from her instrument flowed a haunting but beautiful melody. I recognized it immediately as the one my sister had hummed as a child. It pierced the edges of the auditorium and filled the room from floor to ceiling. Tears flowed, hearts softened, anger fled, and love, like a warm rain, washed over all who heard.

I remembered once struggling with fatherhood and seeking my dad's advice. "What's the secret of being a good father?" I had asked him.

He replied, "Put your hand in the hand of your child's heavenly father and never let go. Then miracles happen."

When Jean Van Olpin had finished, the audience erupted again. As we stood and applauded, I saw Rebe survey the hall. I turned, too. We knew we wouldn't see him, but we felt like we should have. In my mind I chose a place behind guarded curtains where I envisioned Mr. Shimmel clapping and smiling. I imagined my parents standing with him. I reached for Rebe's hand and together we gazed at the room filled with our friends and neighbors. Each had been touched by my father and had come to honor his memory. Each loved Dad for some kindness or for a lifetime of example. Each had beheld his daughter's rare musical gift that night. But only a few knew the price.

As Rebe and I left the auditorium a grateful friend asked me what had made the difference between mediocrity and excellence. I could not respond, but Rebe did. I concurred that it was true.

"The touch of the master's hand," she said. "The touch of the master's hand."

ABOUT THE AUTHOR

Larry Barkdull was a publisher of books, magazines, music, and art prints for twenty years. His first novel, *The Mourning Dove*, won the American Family Institute's Award for Fiction. He lives in Orem, Utah, with his wife and children.